ROADLESS

HOMELANDS

A Collection of Short Stories

By

Baroness Melody Von Smith

Burning
Giraffe

ROADLESS HOMELANDS
Baroness Melody Von Smith

Cover by Jason Helmer

Some of these stories have been published in slightly different form: "The Comic Who Couldn't Laugh" originally appeared on the website On*ce Written*; "The Ocean Doesn't Want Me Today" originally appeared in *Great Lakes Review*; "Yes, This is a Fine Promotion" was originally a short play, produced for the 2011 Buffalo Infringement Festival.

Both "The Comic Who Couldn't Laugh" and "High Price of the Wild Truth" are part of the novel *Survivanoia*.

Admiral of the Red Publishing
Visit our website at www.admiralofthered.com

ISBN-13: 978-0-9981881-1-9
ISBN-10: 0-9981881-1-5

For Gramma

and

for Gir

Contents

Berk

"Pop is dying."

Olmstead's sister breathed these three words through the phone in a regret-filled scratch from rainy Pennsylvania, three thousand miles away.

Olmstead stayed quiet, considered this, listened to the ocean a block outside his door. Eleven years in San Diego had spoiled him. Made him well educated, had him surfing on his lunch breaks. The town he'd grown up in had become a winter wonderland to visit every other Christmas. "Home" had forged itself into a construct propped up by happy letters and punctual holiday cards. Olmstead liked it that way. But some calls must be heeded.

"I'll be there."

Three days later, his red-eye flight touched down at the Pittsburgh airport, and he drove a red, rented Cavalier two hours east and north, back to Berk—both the man and the town.

Berk, Pennsylvania, offered two places to work: the cemetery and the dump. Only it wasn't called the dump anymore, it was the Sanitary Landfill now, and it accepted trash from seven states, with two more scribbling out paperwork even as the town slept.

As Olmstead drove toward Berk the town, he thought of his father, Berkshire Burlington. His father had in fact been named after the settlement by Olmstead's grandfather. Magnus Burlington had brought his wife and little else from Scotland and its abject poverty here to Pennsylvania, where the streets were paved not with gold, but coal. He'd made a happy life for himself and two boys.

Berk Burlington had raised his three kids in the same house he'd been raised. But coal towns wax and wane—in their opportunities, in their wealth, and in their population. Olmstead was one of three, and only his sister had stayed. Waynewright, Olmstead's older brother, had strayed the hundred-some miles to Pittsburgh, but Olmstead, now twenty-nine, had left for California the day he'd graduated high school, fleeing both Berks.

Olmstead's memory had preserved the town in a state of paled but charming splendor. When he'd left, flower baskets lined the sidewalks in the spring, now replaced by autumn pumpkins. He recalled all the shops, the rattling door of Trudy's Hardware, the earthy scent of fresh cut meat at Dean's Deli, and especially the rows of candy in glass jars on the far side of McPherson's drugstore counter. On Saturdays, his father took him there for a malted or a sundae—just him; they'd stop and get candy for his brother and sister before they left. The ice cream, that was a little secret he'd shared with Pop.

Trudy's lay empty, Dean's had become an insurance office, and McPherson's held a for-sale-or-lease sign. Olmstead sighed. But too, he admitted to himself, he felt relieved. Berk wasn't his home. Not anymore. He turned up the car stereo, drove a little faster.

His parents' house lay nine miles past Main Street, on

sixteen acres of never-farmed land. No warning—from his sister or via posted sign, or even a harbinger trail of fugitive refrigerators—nothing alerted him to the state of the house. Later, on the flight home, it would occur to him to wonder why he hadn't worried for the house, given the tragic fate of the town. But just then, Olmstead drove along Highway 22, singing out of tune, passing farms on the left and forest on the right.

At mile seven, the forest gave way to a spatter of bright rectangles separated by chain-link fences—the trailer park. Olmstead's one-time best friend had lived in that trailer park, in space 80. Dillon Mohr. He wondered if Dillon lived in the park now or some place in town, if he had a wife and kids.

The park land butted up against his family's, marked by a line of evergreens. And there it was. On the other side of the pines, stacked sideways and five tall—refrigerators. A wall of refrigerators lined up against the road, like some post-apocalyptic fort. Mostly white, but dotted with the occasional yellow and sometimes sickly green. The house sat on the top of a hill, and all the way up were neat, segregated stacks of metal. Not just fridges, but all types of appliances. Washers, dryers, stoves, dishwashers, cars!

Olmstead heard a horn and realized he'd taken his foot from the gas and now drifted, gaping at the mountain of metal. He waved an apology and brought the rented Chevy back up to speed.

Soon, he spotted the long driveway leading up to his parents' place. But he didn't feel ready to face his family yet. So he drove farther, looking for a different, smaller trail. The one that wrapped around the back of the house and led to the drop-off, by the mine spoils.

A stand of maples marked the far edge of the Burlington property. Half a mile before them, a lengthy tangle of blackberry bushes stretched out from the side of the road, thickening to the shrub-crowded field that had always covered the northeastern side of the property.

Olmstead brought the car to the shoulder, got out and stood peering into the thicket. He fumbled his Oakley sunglasses from the pocket of his suede shirt-jacket, squinting against the deceptively bright sun. The maples stretched stark against a gray backdrop. If he stared hard enough, though, he could make out their buds.

Wind shoved the trees around and cut through his thin suede. Shoulders hunched, he strutted toward the denuded berry bushes—just scruffy, curled sticks now, looking sad and mean as a stray dog. The bushes thinned to a clearing, almost in the center, and beyond that small gap, Olmstead could make out what had once been his trail. He shoved the red-purple arches aside and stepped through them.

Years of neglect had altered a path he once could have traversed on a cloudy midnight. But he made his way. He dodged water-filled ruts now scarring the path, glad he'd worn his chukka boots and not loafers. He and his brother used to ride dirt bikes here in the summer and snowmobiles in winter. Their father had graded it every two weeks, and rode a roller over it every six, to keep it safe for his boys.

Blackberry thorns snatched at his khakis, tore his hands, but Olmstead persevered, his childhood flooding back with each yank of fabric, each scratch dredging up a new memory. What hid back here, he wondered, buried or weathered to nothing? Did the tree house still stand? He and his brother had camped in it for three days during the flood. The safe, the first thing ever illegally dumped on the Burlington property, probably still sat mid-way down the ravine where the mining company's land started.

Olmstead and Dillon had discovered it, and spent the two

weeks of eighth grade spring break beating on it with hammers and a pickax. When it finally gave, they found nothing inside. And they hadn't expected to, really, had made no schemes for spending the treasures. But once it had been cracked, the best friends no longer enjoyed such joint purpose. By summer, they'd both made other friends, only nodding to each other in the hallways once high school started.

The ravine appeared suddenly. Olmstead saw a gash in the landscape where the shrubs and brambles disappeared, and across the gap, only poverty grass grew. The wind coursed again and brought a foul odor from the gully, a stench reminiscent of a restaurant dumpster. When he reached the edge he discovered its source. The ravine, too, was full of junk, like his parents' front hill. But the white goods on his parents' lawn were sorted and salvageable. This was a true trash heap: bald tires, torn clothing, broken lamps, and—Jesus, was that a dead dog?

Olmstead trotted some steps from the edge, an arm over his face so he smelled mostly the suede of his jacket. Satisfied, he supposed. Like the town, the trail betrayed him, charring any idyllic childhood recollections that might have bound him to the place.

As he turned to head back, motion at the far end of the ravine caught his eye. A figure—no, two—emerging from the mine mouth. Two men in boots and jeans and heavy flannels. They both smoked, leaned up against the wood-framed manway. Olmstead recalled stories from his youth of trash heaps catching on fire, and the fires spreading to the mines. The coal seams could light and burn for years. His chest tightened. He should do something! See what these men wanted. They shouldn't be in the mine; it had been closed for years. There were two of them . . . but this was his father's land, at least some of it. He stepped back to the edge of the stinking gully.

Biting laughter flapped out of one of the men. And Olmstead fell backward in time, to a Christmas where he'd needed stitches after being stabbed with scissors, to a summer he'd been pushed off the dock in Florida before he knew how to swim, and to when he'd been shoved out of a tree—and broken his ankle— in Spring of his freshman year. Each time he'd heard that same beating laughter; pitiless—but with a lining of scared apology. It was the sound his brother always made just after doing something wrong.

Olmstead retreated. He jogged through the biting brambles, emerged from the overgrown field, bleeding and confused. In a sudden burst of panic, he craved San Diego. He rested his head against the cold metal of the car. What the hell am I doing? And then his sister's words came back to him: "Pop is dying."

Dying. The significance of his trip sank in. It grabbed him by the belly, and he retched by the side of the road. Gagged up soda and airplane pretzels, then dry heaved—once, twice.

When he was through, he started shivering. Pennsylvania's chill, like his journey's unpleasant purpose, had caught up with him. For eleven years, San Diego's ocean cleansed and freed him. In half an hour, the mountains of his home undid all that with their claustrophobic menace. "I'm from Central Pennsylvania," he used to threaten people. "We eat what we run over." Now he was from Southern California, and the old joke and its threat were on him.

He yearned for the sea and the sun and the vastness of that Western sky, bad-boy blue and endless against the water. Here a mantel of gray held back the sky and its sun. As Olmstead stared into its blankness, the first few flakes of cold wet snow hit his face. He crept back into the rental, rinsed his mouth with Listerine from his overnight bag, and turned the heat up full blast.

* * *

Up the hill, Olmstead's brother's Ford pickup dominated the driveway. Waynewright had parked backwards so the Jolly Roger on the front license plate grinned out. Last Olmstead knew, Waynewright worked as an insurance adjuster in Pittsburgh during the week and came home to his wife and three kids every Friday night. In Olmstead's opinion, the truck proved his suspicion that you can lead a hick to the city, but you can't make him think.

He edged the rental into the space available, rocking from dips in the uneven gravel. How come Pop had never paved the damn driveway? Every year he talked about it. Olmstead had recently offered to pay for it as a Father's Day present. Somehow it hadn't come together.

He took a deep breath and entered the house. The side door led to the kitchen and still needed to be kicked open from the bottom.

"Olmstead!" came his sister's happy bark. And before his boots were even off, two boys in jeans and bright jackets danced around him, circling him. "Uncle Olmstead! Uncle Olmstead's here!" A dizzying flurry of tow-headed Joey, the smaller boy, and his darker-haired, older brother, Luke.

"Can we stay home from school?"

"Nope." His sister pressed lunch boxes—pirates and Star Wars—into their hands and kisses their foreheads.

A dual whine echoed.

"I think maybe your Uncle is staying for more than a few hours. He just might be here when you get home."

Joey's face lit up. "You are?"

"You will?" Luke, the older boy, looked skeptical.

"Unless they throw me out."

"Alright!"

Lilly snapped her fingers, pointed at the door. "Don't miss the bus. I'm not driving you."

"Maybe Uncle Olmstead can drive us."

"Go!"

The boys whirlwinded out.

Olmstead gave his sister a hug, pulled her to her tip-toes.

"It's been way too long," she sighed. She let him go and looked him over, nodded. "You look good."

"You, too."

"I look fat." She pushed her penny-red elbow-length hair into a thick pony tail, wrapping the gum-band from the bread around it.

"Those uniforms probably make everybody look fat."

"These are new. You should have seen the old ones. Pleated pants!"

"Shouldn't you be at work?"

"Nope. They called me off today. Found another body in the fill."

Olmstead eyes widened. Lilly waved an arm. "What do they expect when they handle New Jersey's garbage?" She snagged the collar of his shirt-jacket. "Gimme."

Olmstead relinquished the jacket, wandered around the kitchen and into the living room. "Where is everybody?"

"Wayne took the day off to gallivant with Uncle Devon. The folks are at the doctor."

"At this hour?"

Lilly turned on the faucet, called over the running water. "You know Mama. Their doc is a nut job anyhow! You can schedule a five thirty a.m. appointment with this guy!"

"Old folks' doctor."

"Bingo. Didja eat yet?" Her inquiry carried the unmistakable cadence of the region, with the question sounding after the second-last word: "Didja eat? Yet." Olmstead knew he'd sound the same, without realizing it, in a matter of days. Hickish. Though, he admitted, from Lilly it sounded endearing.

He stooped to read the titles on a collection of animation DVDs. "Nope. They don't feed you on red-eye flights."

"Eggs? Pancakes?"

"What'd the boys have?"

"Some horrible sugary cereal that a better mom wouldn't feed them."

"Sounds great."

The house showed its own signs of wear. But they were cheerful: the DVD rack replaced an old magazine stand, a child-sized desk sat where the coat rack had been. In the mudroom, tiny red and yellow boots stood in line with Pop's black galoshes. Pop was Pap-Pap now. Olmstead knew this intellectually from letters and snapshots. Seeing all the bright children's things in the drab house brought that fact to the inner circle of emotional truth. He smiled.

"Coffee?" called his sister.

"Please." He made his way back to the kitchen. "You live here now."

"Yup."

"What happened to Dale?"

Lilly set a filled coffee cup next to the giant denim-blue bowl and box of Count Chocula. "Gone."

"Like, left? You guys split up?"

She became interested in the acreage beyond the window. "We don't know."

Olmstead poured milk over his marshmallow cereal. "That's a little . . . weird."

Lilly joined him at the table, wrapped both hands around her own oversized blue mug. "Some weird stuff's been going on

9

lately. They wanna re-open the old Howser mine. The one Pop worked in?"

"Yeah?"

"You remember how crazy things got over at the foundry when we were kids? With the union, and the strike, and people's cars vandalized and . . . stuff?"

"And their houses caught fire? Yeah, I remember."

"Some people want this mine. Others don't. Really don't." She frowned at Olmstead, her brown doe eyes questioning: did he honestly remember? "Some of the things people do to try and stop it being opened, you know? Are dangerous."

Olmstead thought of his brother outside the mine mouth. "Like setting fires," he said.

Lilly smiled, convinced. Took a breath like she had plenty to say, but then didn't get to tell him anything more. The door kicked open and there came Uncle Devon, grinning like he'd won money. "Olmy! How's my youngest nephew?"

Olmstead stood and gave his uncle a handshake to half-hug.

Lilly pointed to the muddied floor. "Boots. Boots!"

"Yeah, yeah." He hopped back to the enclosed porch, peeled off his crusty steel-toes. "These ladies and their floors."

Olmstead followed him, looking through the screen door for his brother. "Where's Wayne?"

"He's fixing some girl's fence next door." Devon jerked a thumb at the trailer park, pushed a length of dull, thin hair from his face. He was lean and dirty, his skin permanently grubby from the mines so that even straight from the shower he appeared suspect.

Olmstead glanced at the big black truck still in the driveway. "Did he walk there?"

"Prob'ly took the dirt bike. Or one of the four-wheelers."

Lilly's voice rang from the kitchen: "He oughtta leave that girl alone. He's married and so is she."

Devon flashed his lotto grin, displaying his two gold canines. "Wayne's wife oughtta move down to Pittsburgh, with her husband. Where she belongs." He tromped back into the kitchen, dug through the cupboard for a mug.

"Why?" asked Lilly. "When her husband's chasing poontang right here in Berk?"

Devon laughed to himself. "Anyway, word over at Dew Drop says that girl's old man moved out. He's living in town somewhere. Somewhere classy, like above a pizza joint or something."

Lilly's lips pursed. She shot a sad glance at Olmstead. "That's a damn shame."

Olmstead sensed something he wasn't privy to. Something ominous and ugly beyond his brother's apparent infidelity. "I understand they want to re-open the mine," he blurted.

Devon glared at Lilly before answering. "That's right. Only we don't want it."

"Didn't you work in the mine?" Olmstead asked.

"Right again. So we know how bad it is, me and your Pop. Was us mined it. Along with a thousand other men and a hundred kids. Eighteen inches." He held his hands apart. "That's what they mined down to."

Lilly shook her head. "But this is strip mining, Dev. Nobody has to go inside anything."

"It's the same acid rocks poisoning the water. You wanna be the next Johnstown, where the rivers run orange? You want your kids around the blasting?"

Devon stared out at the acres of stacked trash just like Lilly had. The man's crooked smile revealed little. Olmstead suspected his uncle looked back on those dark days much the way Olmstead recalled grad school. Long nights, impossible tests, teaching classes full of freshmen who didn't care and whose parents threatened him regularly, topped off with the intermittent sleep-deprivation-induced hallucination. But in retrospect those years were fun, challenging. Olmstead missed them.

What did Devon see? Old miners shared the reticence of World War II vets. But sometimes they told stories. Cave-ins, explosions. Glory days.

"Town needs some real jobs," Devon said.

Lilly sighed, sympathetic. "I think we need any jobs we can get. Even mining jobs."

"What you kids don't seem to recall is that Berk was a boomtown. When you were little, this place was growing faster than grass in a rainy summer. They even talked about building a college here! And the mine was already closed then. So why we need it open now?"

Lilly asked the obvious question. "If it was such a boomtown, why'd Pop start collectin' them fridges?"

"Pop's always had those fridges." Olmstead gazed at them, there in the yard. "I mean . . . maybe not so many."

"Not always. Your always maybe," said Lilly, "but not mine or Wayne's."

Uncle Devon swooped a hand, finger aimed, across the vast expanse of dead cars and white goods. "Each one a' them fridges represents fifty bucks."

"And the washers?" Lilly demanded. "And the cars?"

A memory surfaced—Olmstead snapped his fingers. "Pop started taking stuff from people right after the foundry closed. So they wouldn't have to pay the county to come and get it."

"But he charged 'em!" Devon exulted. "Charged 'em, yes, but less than the county did, and people's more likely to give their money to a regular working man tryin' to make a living than to the state." His hooded gaze found Olmstead. "That's how your college got paid, boy."

"That and a number of academic scholarships."

Devon flashed his oblique smile. "You always were an ungrateful sum'bitch."

Olmstead now gestured out the window. "Who's gonna clean up all that crap? That's a veritable Superfund site out there! Pop is dying; guess who's going to foot the bill?"

Berkshire Burlington clattered through the kitchen door. "Who said Pop's dying?" He winked at Olmstead. "Come give your old man a hug, you ungrateful sum'bitch!"

Olmstead threw his arms around his father. He sank his teeth into the flesh inside his cheek to keep from crying, dug his nails deep into his palm to keep from squeezing his Pop the way he wanted, like when he was six. And mostly, he kept his eyes closed.

Berkshire Burlington, always such a broad-shouldered barrel of a man, felt now like a broom in Olmstead's arms. His eyes, molasses black, still sparkled with mischief, but now they did so from the depths of bruisey caverns. When he let go of his son, he leaned back on his cane.

Olmstead coughed away his grief. He couldn't think of anything to say, had forgotten all his obligatory questions about how the surgery went and did the chemo start yet. He panicked that he might throw up again—or worse, start crying—but then he heard the grumble of one of the four-wheelers start up. Not wanting to invoke his uncle's wrath again, he asked instead about the other absent family member. "Where's Mom?"

"Your mother? She's down at the women's club. Thursdays, that's what she does."

Olmstead frowned at his sister. "I thought you said—"

"After Dad goes to the doctor, he drops Mom off at the

club."

Berk glanced at his daughter, then back at Olmstead. "That's right. Drop her off on the way home."

He clattered his way to the kitchen table with his cane and his boots. Same boots as Devon's, Olmstead noticed, but without the steel toes. Berk left a trail of mud, but Lilly didn't bark about it, just wiped it up after him before helping him get the clunky shoes off.

Devon filled a mug halfway with Ensure, then topped it off with coffee. Setting it in the table he asked, "You want some apricots, Berk?"

"Yeah, but I wanna walk around." He smiled at Olmstead, who could only stare into the gray-brown mixture in Berk's mug: his father had always taken his coffee black.

"New way of living, son," Berk grunted, pulling himself to his feet. "It's weird for all of us, not just you." He waved at the table. "Why don't you sit down. You're making me nervous."

Devon yapped something about a cigarette and Lilly echoed his sentiments, but regarding laundry. Suddenly Olmstead was alone with his father.

Berk paced the kitchen, clunk, shuffle, shuffle, taking a dried apricot from the counter on each pass. "Been easier to eat this way since the surgery," he explained. "You send a lot of emails to your mom, kid. Of course I read 'em. But why don't you tell me about California?"

So Olmstead did. He talked about his job and his friends and how much he loved living by the ocean. The University of California at San Diego had provided him a master's degree in computer programming, and the company that hired him straight out of college let him work hours that didn't interfere too much with his surfing.

"We wanted to come for your graduation," his father told

him. "But Lilly was having problems, you know, she had a lump taken out of her breast."

Olmstead's mouth fell open and his brow knitted. "Why didn't anybody tell me!"

"She wouldn't let us." Berk leaned in conspiratorially. "She's glad you got out. Lilly wants out herself, but her husband wouldn't leave. And now she's stuck with me."

His father told him other things, details that don't make it through the filter of three thousand miles: Lilly's older boy was dyslexic but great at math. Olmstead's mother, who had previously refused to take so much as vitamin C, was now on a blood thinner and blood pressure medication. Devon's root canal had gone awry, and so half his face tingled all the time.

His father finished the apricots. "Seems like I'm the healthy one, don't it?" The man's laughter filled any uncomfortable gaps conversation may have left. Olmstead laughed, too. It felt good. Freeing.

Suddenly Lilly was putting rolls and lunch meat—olive loaf, Lebanon bologna, and chipped-chopped ham—on the table, while Devon bitched that there wasn't any beer. Noon already? It seemed to Olmstead that he and his father had just gotten started.

His father eased into the neighboring chair. "We'll talk more later, don't worry."

Devon rinsed Berk's mug out, put ice in it, and was filling it with tap water when a car pulled up outside, catching his attention. "Uhp. Better set another place, Lilly." He grinned over his shoulder at Berk. "Must be noon at the O.K. Corral."

He stood in the foyer with his hand on the doorknob, but waited until the visitor knocked.

"Well look what the cat drug in! How are ya, Officer Mohr?"

"Hiya, Mr. Burlington. I'm sorry to bother yuns at

15

lunchtime—"

"Don't be stupid, boy, you know you're welcome any time." Devon led the uniformed man through the foyer and to the table. "Besides, who makes better coffee than Lilly, huh?"

Olmstead just stared. Dillon Mohr stood—lanky and blonde and pumpkin-headed—like a snapshot from Olmstead's memory. Except for the uniform, which he wore well and with straight-shouldered pride, Dillon could have been visiting from his mom's trailer with a pack of bubble gum and a pocketful of frogs.

He pulled his curvy-brimmed hat off, nodded to Lilly, and shook Berk's hand, all the while apologetically explaining his presence in the same mile-a-minute chatter he'd displayed as a child. "You probably know this already, but it was one of your neighbors that called, so the department figured they better send somebody around to tell you: there's a fire down in the old Howser mine. Looks like it was set right on your property. So of course we need to know if you've seen any . . . " He stopped and stared right back at Olmstead. "Holy shit!"

And, just like when they were kids, Lilly shooed them to the back porch, where they sat on the broad wooden steps eating chipped-chopped ham sandwiches and apples. But instead of finishing off the meal with an Astro Pop, Lilly made them coffees with honey and whipped cream. And though this reminded Olmstead of past arguments whether peanut butter was better with bananas or fluffer-nutter, the two men now spoke carefully, trying to catch up.

"I got married the summer we graduated," Dillon reminded Olmstead. "You don't remember?"

"I wasn't invited."

"I guess you were already in California. 'Course I guess I didn't know that when we were making out the invites . . . " He shrugged. "I dunno why the hell you didn't get an invitation."

"I think we weren't talking."

"Aw. Aw, yeah, huh? What happened?"

"We opened an empty safe."

Dillon nodded once. "That's right." He gazed toward the maples, where they'd worked over that dumped safe for ten days. "Nothing inside," he said, pensive. A lull. Then: "Your sister's being promoted to shift supervisor. Did she tell you?"

"Yeah, I heard. Something about landfill mining?"

"It's new. They rework 'em and and get the good stuff out, then I guess they can use the leftover space. Doubles the life of the fill, apparently. They put her in charge of all that."

"Did she go back to school?" Just how much did Olmstead not know?

"Naw, I guess there's some training program or certification? Something." Dillon fished a circular container from his back pocket, pulled a small white pouch from it. "It's great 'cause it will double the crew, too, at least on first shift." He tucked the pouch between his cheek and gum, dropping his voice. "Maybe she can even get your scruffy old uncle a job. He's more of a problem since he quit drinking than he was when we were kids!"

Olmstead recalled his uncle's angry quest for beer at lunch. "You sure he quit?"

"Yeah, this week. I can tell from his temper. He's way less ornery when he falls off the wagon. Probably 'cause when he's sober he only hangs with Snail an' nem. Remember Snail?"

"Moose's cousin?"

"Yup."

Olmstead put up a hand. "Say no more. Surprised they haven't all shot each other."

Dillon laughed in agreement. "So, how long you back for?"

Olmstead shrugged. "As long as it takes."

"You in charge of your pop's estate?"

"Cleaning all this up, you mean?"

Dillon squinted, puzzled, then guffawed. "Cleaning it up?"

Olmstead nodded, gazing out at the mountains of metal. "That's my reaction, too."

"No, you don't get it. Your Uncle an' nem bought a shredder, and hitched up with, I dunno, some company that's separating the stuff. The government paid for the shredder, I guess so's they'd agree to recycle the mercury? But that"—he waved a finger at the yard of junk—"that's worth, I don't even know. More than I'll make in my lifetime, anyway."

Olmsted started to laugh but stopped himself. "Are you serious?"

"Yeah! I can't believe they didn't tell you."

Olmstead considered his uncle. "I can." The thought irritated him, so he changed the subject. "You still living in the park?"

Dillon sort of scoffed. "Nope. My wife is, though, and my two little girls."

"She got the property, huh?"

"I gave it to her." Dillon shrugged. "I don't hate her or nothing. We actually have a lot of fun together still. Ballgames an' nat? We're friends."

Dillon was ingenuous enough for this to be a truth. "So where are you living?" Olmstead asked.

"Just moved into town. Above a pizza shop."

Olmstead looked away. He sat next to his once-best friend thinking about how he was going to kick the shit out of his brother when he saw him, and then a stray thought spilled clear from his head out of his mouth: "Did my Pop set that fire?"

Dillon smiled but his brow creased. "Are you for real asking me this?"

Olmstead shook his head, fearing he'd just ratted out his old man.

Dillon laughed, punching Olmstead in the arm. "The whole town knows your father set them fires. Hell, three counties over they knew, before the fires even started!" He shrugged. "What are we going to do, prosecute a dying man? He won't live through the trial. Why wreck his last days?" He shrugged again. "Not to be mean. Sorry."

Olmstead waved the comment away.

Silence settled between them, but this time warm and comfortable, like a fire on a chilly summer night. Olmstead closed his eyes and recalled days of tadpoles and skinned knees, nights of fireflies and s'mores. He couldn't help but smile.

Berk was now a landfill; Berkshire's house, a dump. But years ago, when Olmstead had been raised in it, the town had been a good place to be raised. And the man had been a good father. Still was.

"Maybe it doesn't doom us to love where we've come from." This too spilled out of Olmstead's head, and he said it to himself. But of course Dillon was there with him, to hear it.

His childhood friend shielded his eyes with a hand, looked to the trailer park where his kids were growing up that very moment. "Man, I sure hope not!"

Olmstead sat back, sipped Lilly's sweet coffee. Glad he'd heeded the call.

The Comic Who Couldn't Laugh

Benjamin Myers, wearing only his boxers, stood in the entrance of his bungalow scratching his head and squinting at the man on his doorstep. Trees above blazed bronze in the early morning sun. The still air, thick and stale, promised triple digits by noon and held tantalizing scents of breakfast—sausage!—from the cafés on Melrose Avenue, half a block away.

The man who'd pounded on Ben's door, dragging him to wakefulness, looked to Ben like he could use some breakfast. Despite his nervous eyes and flaring nostrils, though, this lean stranger had the face of a handsome boxer. Semi-famous, certainly. Mid-list? Maybe porn. Probably not, though, with that shock of gray. Where'd I see this guy? Ben wondered.

He realized the man was talking—apparently had been.

"I'm sorry, what?"

The man sighed, shoved a hand at Ben. "This is yours."

The hand held a wallet—black and worn.

"I don't think so," Ben started. He glanced toward the bedroom where his black linen trousers lay folded over a chair. Was his wallet in them? Wasn't his wallet brown? Maybe he should check. But the prospects of leaving this wild-eyed, disheveled man alone at the threshold disconcerted him.

The man made his decision for him. "The address is yours! Take it. Take it!" He yanked Ben's hand from its akimbo post, shoved the wallet into it and fled.

Ben slammed the door. He peered through the slats of his wooden blinds but didn't see the man, or hear a car leave, just the murmur of early yuppies and ambitious tourists.

In the kitchen, the sun's sharp angle told him it couldn't be past eight. Far too early for a bartender whose shift ended at 2:30, and had stumbled through the door—womanless—at quarter past 7, to be up.

But curiosity overrode tiredness. He reheated a cup of yesterday's coffee and opened the wallet. Its license was in one of those flip-out plastic things. The address indeed matched Ben's. Ben didn't recognize the guy in the photo, but he'd bought the house from someone who had rented it out, so this must have been one of the previous tenants. Examining the picture, he decided that the madman at the doorstep must have been either blind or incredibly generous in his physical assessments. This photo guy shared the wallet bearering-stranger's high-cheekboned face, but offset by blue eyes and red hair. Not gray, as Ben's had turned, nearly completely as of last year, betraying him at the comparatively young age of thirty-four. Women described Ben as "cute," sometimes "handsome," but he'd never graduated to sexy.

The microwave beeped. On his way to it, he yanked closed the curtains over the kitchen sink. Who was this previous tenant guy? Ed Bloodworth. Even his name was creepy!

Despite feeling voyeuristic, Ben riffled through the rest of the wallet. Not much in it, no Norton's Food card, no library card, no photos. A bank card, maybe he could drop the wallet off at BankZilla and they could hunt Ed down. What unnerved

Ben was the money. Hundred dollar bills. Lots of them. And some weird orange certificate things. Foreign currency? Ben felt uncomfortable touching them. He thought about calling 411, but what could he tell the guy if he did find him? No, dropping it off at the bank seemed better. Good and anonymous.

He left the wallet on his dresser. Some superstitious feeling made him check his pants, make sure he still had his own wallet, his own identification, was still Ben Myers.

He took a shower, mostly cold. The cool water left him refreshed and sleepy, so he went back to bed. At three, his clock radio came on, the Clash pulling him from sleep. Thursday. Thursdays meant the comedy club. In lieu of the linen pants, he dug a pair of brown, wide-wale cords from his drawer and put on a brick-red jersey-cut T-shirt. Safe, earth colors. The cut of the shirt hid his little teddy-bear belly. The fact of the colors and cut, that he knew this and didn't mind, made Ben feel old.

* * *

Busta Guts: "Food and Funny, See?" The sign featured a typecast mobster, smoking a fat cigar and rubbing his belly as he laughed. In fact, the drawing was a caricature of Buster DelGrosso, the unfunny-comic-but-shrewd-businessman who owned the place. Back in the 80s, when stand-up had reached its pinnacle, Busta's provided the brightest new talent to the screen. Now it lived off its reputation, and like so many places in Hollywood, was frequented mostly by tourists. Though as of late, stand-up seemed positioned for a comeback, and the Home Piracy Network had begun filming their half-hour specials of up-and-coming comics at Busta's—including one tonight—so who knew?

The girl showed up early, but that wasn't the only reason

she stood out. People dressed tourist-nice at Busta's, khakis and pressed shirts. This chick had on a baseball jersey—Pitt—over a short plaid skirt and boots. Plaid boots—British combat style—with gold laces that matched the writing on the jersey. Underneath the skirt were black fishnet stockings, and she wore the jersey open at the top, revealing a lace tank top.

Just enough skin, Ben thought. He hoped she didn't come near him. She did, of course.

"Bar open yet?"

"Only for you." Geez what a cliché! Ben wanted to slap himself.

"What's your special?"

"What's you pleasure?"

Her ice-blue eyes sparkled. "I asked you first."

Ben faltered. He wasn't supposed to serve his personalized drinks here. But no one else was around yet, he wouldn't be upstaging anybody . . .

He leaned in conspiratorially. "Sweet or sharp?"

"What?"

"If you had to choose between, say, Jaeger Meister and peach Schnapps, which would it be?"

"Jaeger."

That meant he could make her a sit-and-spin. He selected a pilsner glass, poured a half gin, half vodka base (mixed over ice), and two magical liquors that sat on top of each other, one blue, one red. He set it in front of the girl, inserted a stirrer. "Watch."

He stirred it with vigor. The drink swirled and turned patriot blue. It kept spinning and the blue faded, passed to purple for just a moment, then flushed fire-engine red.

The girl grinned, cocked her head of loose black curls and examined him. "You work at Tattoo."

"Maybe."

"He does," said a different woman, a swank redhead. "He makes another drink called the Kafka. It's gray and a little city forms at the bottom, disappears each time you take a sip, then reforms again, reconfigured." She dropped onto a stool and shot him a smile. "He also juggles broken bottles and breathes fire."

"Hello, Heather." Ben sort of smirked, like a fond older brother. "What'll it be?"

"The usual. And: Lacy was prowling around here earlier."

"I thought Buster banned that crowd."

"He doesn't know Lacy hawks, he thinks she's just a starlet. Besides she was prowling around for you." Heather turned to Ben's new friend. "Comedy is like acting; the porno industry snatches up the failures. Eats them up and shits them out." She aimed her smarmy smile at the girl. "Are you on tonight?"

Ben glared at Heather. "I'd introduce you two, but I don't know Pitt's name. This is Heather."

The girl put out a hand. Ben prepared Heather's whiskey sour, glad for the respite. The pornography hawks made him prickle. They stalked joints like Busta's, made good-sounding offers to fame-starved kids, "Hey baby, you're gorgeous, you're talented, you could make three hundred bucks a day—working in film!" Buster had cracked some guy's skull open one night and promised next time to shoot him. So what was Lacy chasing?

Ben set Heather's drink on a napkin.

"Her name is Chloe," Heather told him, and pranced off.

After Heather left, Chloe asked him, "Your girlfriend?"

"Absolutely not."

"She'd like to be." She eyed him over. "And . . . you've slept with her."

Ben felt himself flush. "Only once. We were both drunk."

"Maybe you'd like to get drunk with me some time."

Ben's face absolutely burned. He pointed to Chloe's jersey.

"Did you go to Pitt?"

"No."

"Oh. I thought maybe you did because of the shirt. That's where I'm from."

"I bought this in Venice. I thought it was funny, you know, to buy a Pittsburgh shirt in California."

"Funny peculiar, or funny haha?"

"Funny ironic." She sipped her sit-and-spin.

"You ever been there?"

"You couldn't pay me enough."

"How do you know if you've never been?"

"Let's just say Pittsburgh is aptly named."

"You're pretty funny." He gazed at her suspiciously. "Are you on tonight?"

"No, one of my friends is. Vonnie."

"Connie Anders?"

Chloe shook her head. "Vonnie. Upchurch."

Ben nodded, pursed his lips slightly, hoping he disguised how impressed he was. And jealous. Upchurch was the headline, the one whose special was being filmed. Former wife of rap-rock star Bagga Chips, comedienne Upchurch had taken the horrific and slanderous lyrics he'd sung about her and twisted them against him. Now half the country laughed at him. Naturally, this had gained her quick access to the talk-show circuit. Brilliant. Ben wished he'd thought up some similar approach with his own, now long-abandoned shtick.

"Want to meet her?" Chloe asked.

This struck Ben as an odd question, being that he worked for the club and it was usually him asking that question, kind of a standard pick-up line, come to think of it. "Sure."

"Good. We can all have dinner at my place Saturday night. Good?"

"Uh . . . good!"

Any fantasies he may have harbored about sex with two girls—one of them a famous comic!—or watching two girls have sex with each other, were squelched by Heather as they closed up.

"Neither of those women even wants to see you naked. I, on the other hand . . ."

"You realize that, since you're the club manager, I could potentially sue you for sexual harassment." He winked at her.

"Oh please do. Court would at least break the predictable cycle that has become my life. Seriously—Honey? Use a condom."

* * *

Before Chloe had the door open she apologized to Ben. "Vonnie couldn't make it."

"I'm not surprised. Saturday is top dollar for a comic."

"I didn't think you'd make it either, mister bartender."

"Speaking of which." He shoved a bottle of wine at her. "That's from Canada," he said. "Eastern Canada."

"I didn't tell you what I was making."

"So?"

"So how did you know what wine to get?"

He grinned. "I'm a bartender."

Chloe had a nice apartment in a marginal neighborhood, on the seedier side of Hollywood. Maybe the vaulted ceilings and hardwood floors made up for not being able to leave the house after dark without putting on some hardcore attitude.

She sat him at the dining room table, wrought iron with an inset gray marble top. Ben ran a hand along it. "This is gorgeous."

"Thrift store, can you believe it?"

In place of a tablecloth which would have covered the beauty of the marble, she'd draped three cobalt blue runners. A metal watering can spilling over with blue and white irises rested on the farthest of these, and cloth napkins set beside placemats graced the other end. Tasteful.

And the food! Duck prepared in Grand Marnier sauce, with wild rice and perfectly steamed asparagus. Crème brûlée for dessert. Chloe owned a cook's blowtorch. Ben thought he could marry this girl. She had taste, a sense of humor and cooked like a fiend!

"Why are you such a good cook?"

"Why?"

"You have to admit it's a bit unusual for somebody, what, twenty-five?"

"Is this an elaborate ruse to determine my age?"

"Yes."

"I'm twenty-nine."

Ben finished his wine. "That's still your twenties. Not many people in their twenties cook this well unless it's their profession."

"I'm not a chef."

"I figured. So?"

"I watched Food TV a lot."

Ben sensed there was more. For the first time in their short relationship, Chloe seemed hesitant. He hedged the bet: "For a reason?"

"Do you really want to know?" She attempted a laugh. "In the past five years, my life became a bad made-for-cable movie. Oh wait, that's a redundancy."

He snickered. "But yeah, I'd really like to know."

"My dad died when the World Trade Center came down. All the channels were showing it all the time. I couldn't get away from it, but I couldn't stand the silence when the TV was off. Music wasn't enough. I wanted voices, you know? People."

Ben searched her for signs of farce—was he being punked?

He didn't think so. Her speech was rushed. Plus the way she'd referred to it, not the media-catchy 9-11.

"What about the Weather Channel?" he asked.

Chloe shook her head. "It affected the weather. All that smoke and debris? So I started to watch all these different people cook. It got to be interesting. They each have their own little pet thing. And cooking, it's a form of creation I guess." She shrugged. "I found it therapeutic. Don't laugh."

He looked at her, sparkling eyes and wide smile; Chloe was struggling not to laugh herself.

"How about your mom?"

"Died a year later. Of a broken heart."

"That's poetic." He instantly regretted his sarcasm.

"It seems to frighten people less than telling them she hung herself from the exposed pipes in the basement."

"I . . . I'm sorry."

Chloe glared at him only for a moment, then shrugged again. "I warned you." So what about you? Any after-school specials you want to share?"

Ben rubbed his chin. "We'll do me next time."

"I won't do you next time. I'm a third date girl."

* * *

Ben drove home happy, not even minding his broken radio. Brand new car and the radio—satellite—stopped working after two weeks. The dealer said it wasn't their responsibility. Here's a voucher, go to a stereo place. The stereo place looked sideways at the car because it was a hybrid and they don't work on hybrids 'cuz it's an electric car, comprende? They could be electro-cuted.

But he wasn't thinking about any of that. He was humming and dreaming about Tuesday, his scheduled second date. How foresightful of him to have taken those passes to Alrik's art show opening. He never believed he'd actually use them, but stuff like that can come in handy. No pun intended, he joked to himself, then remembered it's the third date he had to get to before there'd be any hands involved. He already knew just where to take her. As such a good cook, she'd be hard to impress, but in searching for hard-to-find wines, he'd recently stumbled across this Romanian place and—who was parked in his driveway?

A silver Escalade sat, motor running, across his driveway so that it blocked his entrance. Adrenaline brought Ben its rush of anger and irrationality. Then he noticed that one of the taillights was out, and sighed. Heather.

For show, he screeched to a halt inches from her bumper and tossed open the door. He had not been completely truthful with Chloe. Yes, he and Heather hooked up only once, but neither of them was drunk, and it was the beginning of an arrangement whereby if both of them were free and physically needy they could use each other to fill that need. Technically, he was not yet with anybody. Chloe's chastity was cute, though; he found it charming, and he'd decided before he got out of his car to send Heather home.

But as he stepped from his hybrid, the Escalade darted away with a tight squeak of tires. Ben cursed after the SUV, suddenly bitter with the realization that he'd just been blue-balled twice in one night.

*　*　*

"So how was your wild night, loverboy?"

"You should know."

Heather raised her eyebrows at him. "How's that?"

"I appreciate our arrangement, but I'm dating. And color

me crazy, but stalkers make me nervous."

"What on god's green earth are you on about?"

Ben peered at his manager. She had a hand on her tilted hip and a vaguely-offended sort of frown creased her brow.

"Don't you drive a silver Escalade with a burned out taillight?"

"Silver Explorer, psycho. Cadillac makes Escalade. And I fixed my busted taillight two weeks ago. You told me where to go."

That's right, he had. So who the hell'd been parked outside his house? Like they were casing the place. Not that Ben had much, necessarily, but he liked the things he did have. His couch was comfortable, his stereo kicked ass, and the bedroom furniture had been his grandmother's, which in his opinion more than made up for the dresser's mismatched hardware and circular stains. He'd considered refinishing the piece but—the wallet! Shit, he'd forgotten all about it.

What if the Escalade guy was Ed the Wallet Owner? Ben took a deep breath. Tomorrow the banks would be open. He'd return it. He counted his drawer, liquor and receipts, brought the numbers back to Heather along with an apology. She shrugged in a way that told him she was still irritated, but gave him her usual "Break a leg at Ta-Twat."

Ben hated Club Tattoo but loved working there. The clientele ranged from over-privileged children-of-famous-people to Persian princes and their bombshell American dates. They had a stage show on the lower level—impersonators, magic, sometimes vaudevillian stuff. Upstairs, people danced. No average citizens and no white light ever graced the carpets, dance floors or bathrooms of the infamous Club Tattoo. Their bouncers carried side arms. More than one of their waiters were rumored to have used their kitchen torches for things beyond the showy at-the-table caramelization of desserts, and two of the waitresses were known for going on to become Hollywood Madams. For Ben, all this meant two things: that he got to put on a show and that he got tipped superbly.

What Heather had told Chloe was true—the fire breathing and broken bottles. He also worked some basic magic: a cup-and-ball trick he did with shot glasses and maraschino cherries, a dollar-in-the-lemon trick. This week he planned to debut a disappearing dollar bit. "Drink Your Money Away," he'd named it. He poured a shot with the money in the glass, still visible when served. Once the patron consumed it, the cash disappeared. Ben made out on money tricks because Tattoo customers seldom carried anything smaller than tens, and they usually let him keep the bill.

The ninth dollar-drinker shook his shot glass, stared into the bottom, rubbed his finger around the inside.

"Amazing, isn't it?" a girl asked.

A girl with black hair and ice blue eyes. "Chloe!"

"I've been sitting here for nearly ten minutes. What's wrong, you don't recognize me out of uniform?"

The Ninth Guy barked, "Hey! Where's my Abe?"

Ben pulled a five dollar bill out of the guy's ear, handed it to him. The guy snatched it and waltzed away.

Ben frowned after him. Chloe reached around him for a handful of maraschino cherries. "Cheap SOB, huh?"

"Naw, I lost concentration at the end there. It's all about timing." He noticed the cherries, aimed his frown at her.

"Is that your way of saying scram? Get outta here kid, you bother me?"

He blinked at her. "No. Don't eat those, I have to account for them." He snagged one from her. "You're probably right, cheap SOB. So, come here often?"

"Hey Benjy Boy!" A leggy platinum blonde poured herself into a stool at the bar's far end. Veins bulged through the loose skin of her hands, but her face could still sell lip gloss to teeny-boppers.

Ben waved a finger at Chloe—"Just a minute"— and moved to the blonde. "What's your poison, Geena?"

"What, no kiss? Give Mamma a kissy-wissy, baby." She yanked him to her by his shirt, took his face in both her hands and planted a sloppy kiss on his mouth. Amazingly, she left no traces of lipstick. "I hear you're making dollar bills disappear tonight."

"I hear you're making other things disappear."

Geena giggled. "Show me yours. Sorry, but you can't afford mine."

Ben poured her a shot, the money disappeared, he pulled it out of her blonde mane. She let him keep the bill, and hers was a twenty. He served the small crowd that Geena inevitably left in her wake. Eventually everybody had something in his hand, and Ben returned to Chloe.

"You here alone?"

"Vonnie dragged me. She almost fits in around here."

"She doesn't have a gig tonight?"

Chloe nodded. "Late. Up on the Strip somewhere."

Ben wondered if Chloe got paid to act as her friend's mascot, but before he'd figured a tactful way to phrase this question, Lionel burst through the swing doors behind the bar. "Heads up! Ice! Ice, ice, baby!" He dumped a plastic busboy's tray-load of ice into the bar trough, muscles bulging around his white tank undershirt. "You short anything else?"

"I could use more Blue Curacao," Ben said. "And don't eat those!" He smacked Lionel's hand, which was full of bright red cherries.

"Uh-oh." Lionel sang.

"What?" Ben followed the bar back's gaze. "Oh."

"Porno mafia at three o'clock."

"Why does Alex let them through the door?"

"And the fetish crew, no less."

Two women and three men reached the top of the stairs, spread like a survey crew, like they owned the joint. Or planned to rob it. They'd've been awfully conspicuous though. Two of the three men had slick black ponytails and black leather trench coats. The third guy's dirty blonde hair fell into his eyes. He also wore leather—a motorcycle jacket over a Hawaiian shirt—and had an eyebrow ring and a goatee.

Then there were the women. One like Elvira but with breasts the size of watermelons. On her arm, a small, skinny girl in a plush fur leopard top and matching boyshort panties. She had boots to her knees, Halloween cat-ears over her black Betty Page cut, and wore a mesh duster that trailed on the floor. Her chest held mere cantaloupes.

Ben turned to Chloe to tell her about how the last time this crew showed up, they'd had to close the floor for a night to clean up the mess. Luckily, the club appealed to a crowd made hot by scandal and murder, especially if the death involved being smothered between watermelon tits.

But Chloe had slid off her stool and was creeping toward the women's bathroom, eyes set on the youngest of the men, the one with the short hair.

Lionel came swinging back through the doors again. "Boss says blow."

"Really?"

"Yeah, apparently these clowns crashed the gates. Riley's on his way up, says get everybody out, don't come back till tomorrow."

"Who's gonna finish my shift?"

Lionel shrugged. "My guess is Tattoo's second floor is closing for the evening."

"My guess is Riley sets this shit up."

Ben searched for Chloe but to no avail, decided she was holed up in the bathroom with her comedienne friend and he'd call her later. He considered hitting Peanuts or one of the other dance clubs, but realized he was bored with that scene, was very much looking forward to Tuesday night with Chloe and the prospect of Tattoo being reduced to just a job, from the slender-possibility-palace he currently pretended it wasn't. So, for the first night in many months, Ben headed straight home after work.

As he pulled into his driveway, his headlights swept over his little house, revealing the unmistakable form of a person standing in his front room. Forgetting the public service announcements recommending that, should you come home to find a stranger in your house, you go to another house and phone the police, Ben burst from his still-running car and lunged through the door. A shadow slipped through his sliding kitchen door. Ben followed. In the backyard, he saw someone hop at the eight-foot rock wall, struggle for a grip. He lurched after the intruder. But lack of exercise got the best of him. He stood panting and sweating in the dim light as the figure slipped lithely into the neighbor's garden.

Ben put his car in the garage and headed inside to assess the damage. The lock was busted, but nothing in the house appeared broken or missing. Perhaps he'd had the good fortune to arrive just in time? He checked the bedroom, where even the foisted mystery wallet still sat unmolested on his dresser.

But there'd been a sound as the intruder slipped over the wall, the unmistakable crunchy squeak of leather. Only certain types of people, Ben knew, wore a leather jacket in midsummer. The same kinds of people, come to think of it, who were likely to drive silver Cadillac SUVs. This, on the same night as the Porno cartel? This was bad.

Ben didn't want to end up like the stupid amateurs trying to make it in the business. The hawks always collected a few failed actors who didn't mind, maybe liked the work. Maybe tried to get a little too big. Like any big-money business, competition killed. The Porn kings and queens regularly met up with people at Tattoo, usually men, who left the club with them and then disappeared for good. Occasionally they didn't leave the club at all. Then the Tattoo staff got to clean up the mess.

Yeah, this was bad.

Ben slept in his clothes. At seven-thirty his alarm went off, but he needn't have set it—he'd been awake since dawn, staring out the window and trying to keep his heartrate close to normal. He paced outside BankZilla, panting like a rabid dog for the three minutes it took them to unlock the door to customers.

The aging, too-skinny clerk drew away from him slightly, as if he smelled. Her eyebrows, which she had shaved and painted back on so that she appeared perpetually surprised, made Ben slightly afraid of her and indeed of the bank, as if he had walked into an elaborate trap.

"This is—I found this. And I have reason to believe the man it belongs to needs it very much." He explained about the address, slid the wallet under the shield of bulletproof plastic.

False-nailed fingers snatched the wallet from the metal tray and tapped a keyboard furiously. Still gazing at her computer screen, Creepy Bank Lady shook her head. "Account's closed. Has been for months. The last address we have is yours."

"What can I do?" Ben's vision tunneled.

"Try the DMV. Next in line, please."

"His license has my address."

"Then four-one-one. Next!"

He stumbled punch-drunk out of the chilly bank and into the bright morning heat of an LA Monday. For a while he sat with his car running, relearning how to breathe. And sweating. The heat made him come to. He raised a hand to his new car's air conditioner vent, discovered it pumped out damp, tepid air.

Ben sighed. "Alright," he said out loud to himself. "Fine. Four-one-one it is." He headed one block north to the Honda of Hollywood dealer. "Why not confront Bloodworth directly?" he shouted at himself. "These people already know where I live anyway, right? Right! If they want to kill me, they will." His arms flailed in surrender, briefly abandoning the steering wheel. "With some luck I'll wake up while they're hovering over my bed with a butcher knife and just hand them the wallet."

He ran a red light and stop sign, and cut off an old lady.

Perhaps the Honda dealer manager perceived that he was contending with a man on the edge. It took very little to convince him that, unlike the stereo, the AC was certainly their responsibility, and they would see what they could do right this minute.

While Ben was waiting, he used the manager's phone.

"Information. What city?"

But after some key-tapping she told him, "No listing in the greater Los Angeles area."

He hung up to find the dealership manager looking apologetic and a little frightened.

"Let me guess," Ben said. "You need a part."

The manager nodded. "If you'd like you can take the car today and drop it off again. We should have it by tomorrow."

"No, take it. Keep it. Call me when it's ready. If I'm not dead, I'll come get it."

* * *

Tuesday evening the sun retreated but left its heat behind. At seven, the buildings blazed metallic in the low light, and the temperature still hung in the high nineties. Ben phoned Chloe, left a message: Could she drive tonight?

Nobody threatening had shown up at Busta Guts, and Ben had spent the night on Heather's couch. He considered asking Chloe to pick him up from the club, but he needed of a change of clothes, and the tickets for the art show, which he hoped he remembered correctly as being tacked to his bulletin board.

Back at his little house, nothing seemed amiss, making him wonder if conspiracy theories had finally taken over his better judgment. He heard the phone ring from the shower and found Chloe's voice on his machine when he got out. "My AC is broken too. So's my stereo. But I can drive if you want."

At nine precisely, Chloe pulled up in her yellow Volkswagen Golf, wearing a mint green slip dress, a black feather boa and black vinyl platforms. The stereo, to Ben, seemed healthy enough, blasting 80s favorites loud enough to rattle his front windows. But he had more pressing things weighing on his mind.

"Listen!" he hollered over a Duran Duran tune he was embarrassed to admit still made him choke up if he paid attention. "I hope you didn't split the other night because of Lana!"

Chloe shook her head, made a right onto Melrose.

"Or Josie!"

She shook her head again.

"Can I turn this down!"

"It doesn't turn down!"

Very funny, Ben thought. If she was pissed at him, why hadn't she said so earlier? He punched the down arrow, furious. There was no way he was showing up at his friend's art opening with some chick who—it didn't turn down. It also didn't turn off, and the next song was Led Zeppelin, which probably ranked as Ben's most hated band ever, but he couldn't change the station either.

"Your radio's broken!"

"I told you that! I also have to turn the heat on now, or the engine's going to overheat!"

Ben trusted things could only get better.

His friend's opening ran out of a one-room independent gallery in Studio City, in the Valley. Chloe found a parking space in the bank lot across the street. When she turned the engine off, and the full-blast heater and killer radio with it, Ben stumbled out of the car into the comparatively cool air and pretended to kiss the ground.

Chloe stood, arms crossed. "You can take a taxi home."

"I think it might be worth it. How can you drive that thing?"

"It's been broken forever; I'm used to it. Besides, how else were we supposed to get here?"

Ben stood, dipped his head. "Point taken."

"Can we go see some art now, please?"

"Well, I can't promise you that." He took her arm and led her across Ventura Boulevard to Gallery AnArtChy.

Music poured from inside the tiny, bright gallery. "Sounds like they hired the Flintstones band to play," Ben said.

"I like it. That's a marimba. The marimba is a great instrument because it can be simultaneously spooky and whimsical. Unlike the poor Theremin, which is always associated with monsters around the corner."

"Thank you, professor."

"Don't mention it."

Inside, amidst the brilliant lights and dazzling paintings, Ben found his friend, the artist, Alrik. Despite the man's Scandinavian name, he stood less than six feet, talked like a surfer, and had trim, dark hair that would have looked absurd underneath a Viking helmet. His paintings, too, were quintessentially American, a high-energy blend of comic book and graffiti art. Not "moving" or poignant perhaps, but an awful lot of fun.

Chloe assembled a cheese and fruit plate for them to share, and Alrik pressed plastic goblets of wine into both their hands. But he pulled Ben aside, "There was a guy here asking about you, man. I mean he was looking for somebody else, but asked about you too. You know some guy name a' . . . Blood . . . something?"

Ben's stomach tightened. "Was this guy in a leather coat?"

"Naw, business clothes. Blonde hair, goatee. He left a card."

"Did he say what he wanted?"

Alrik shook his head. "Something about owing him money." He handed Ben a card, which Ben surreptitiously pocketed.

"Did he seem . . . dangerous?"

His friend shrugged. "It's hard to be dangerous in a Hugo Boss suit." He sent Ben to view the show.

Ben gulped his wine, snagged another glass. He scrutinized the other visitors. They seemed divided into a blend of hip kids and Euro-trash. The kids were skinny, had spiky hair bleached at the tips, or no hair and goatees. They wore Glitter Baby and Hip-Hop-HurRave gear, greeted the artist with congratulatory hugs, wolfed cheese, shied away from the wine. The others— older, darker—frowned at them. Frowned at the art. They leaned into each other to whisper in foreign snatches, broke apart in nasty laughter.

"Know any of those clowns?" Chloe asked. "They look like they got lost on their way to Tattoo."

"Listen, I hope you didn't split on Sunday because of that woman at the bar. Or the chick in the cat suit."

"None of the above. One of those guys? Was my boss."

"I thought you work in an office."

"I'm not saying I can account for it, I'm just telling you why I left."

"What's the name of your company again?"

"Why, you think I'm lying? That I'm actually a porn star?"

"No. If you were, you'd have a nicer car."

"Those girls make a lot, huh?" She sounded like she might be considering it in earnest.

Ben wanted to avoid a public hard-on. "Want to go?"

"I guess. Where?"

"Are you hungry?" he asked.

"I could eat."

"There's this weird place I stumbled on, Romanian food. I was going to wait until Saturday to take you—"

"But we seem to need something to occupy us."

Ben nodded, feeling warm from the wine. "Occupy. Exactly."

"What is Romanian food?"

He led her back across Ventura to the car. "I have no idea. I thought you'd know. You're the chef."

"Dracula was from Romania. Maybe they'll have blood pudding."

She started the car, killing the conversation.

The restaurant proved elusive, having no sign. But an odd building housed it, a long white box with a sharp peaked roof.

Chloe stepped out of the car and looked around. "I have no idea where we are."

Ben pointed up the road. "Three blocks that way is the 110-105 interchange."

Inside was cool and cozy. A brunette, college-age girl sat in front of a register, hopped off her stool when Ben and Chloe entered. "Welcome to Vlad's!" She gave them a warm smile.

"I love your dress!" Chloe spouted in admiration of the girl's floor-length black and purple velvet gown. The top fit like a vest, while the bottom belled.

"Thanks! My Gramma made it."

She led them to the main room, where two men crouched over a chess game. An enormous black dog slept under the table. Aside from them, Ben and Chloe were the only customers.

The girl sat them at the table farthest from the concentrating men, explained the menu and made suggestions in good, only slightly accented English. While she was talking, an older gentleman wearing shirt sleeves and an apron snuck around her and set a basket of warm bread on the table.

"Take your time. Let me know if you have questions."

Ben set the menu aside. "Apparently Romanian food is organ meats, wine and vodka. And bread."

Chloe broke the loaf into two large chunks. "Our question has been answered."

"Ours has, but mine hasn't."

"What?"

"You never told me where you work."

"I did so, on our first date."

"Tell me again."

The girl brought a bottle of wine, performed an elegant ceremony of opening it in front of them and letting them smell the cork, giving them just enough in the glass to obtain their approval before leaving them the bottle.

"Survivanoia," Chloe told him once the waitress had left.

Ben snapped his fingers. "Ah! I knew it was something intense like that. Inside sales, right?"

"Right."

"See, I was listening. I just suffer from short-term memory loss."

"So if I ask you next week, you'll remember?"

"You're pretty funny."

"You say that a lot, are you aware? But you never laugh at anything I say. You don't even smile, you just give me this sort of smirk."

Ben gave just the smirk she spoke of. "That's my after-school special, as you termed it."

"Go on, I'm tuned in. I've got popcorn and everything. Even better, I've got wine."

"Really good wine, too." He helped himself to another glass. "Okay . . . I came here from Pittsburgh to do comedy. Believe it or not, Pittsburgh has a good reputation, comedy-wise."

"Vonnie confirms that, yes."

"I did pretty good out there, and I don't have that Pittsburgh accent—"

"True. You haven't said 'yuns' or 'Stillers' once since I met you."

"—so I figured I had a shot. I come out here and I'm doing alright, playing places like Adlibs, and getting good reviews and a word here and there from some bigger names."

"And then—tragedy struck." Chloe mimicked a violin.

Ben tossed back the rest of his wine. He told her about how his taste buds went funny on him one day, apples tasted salty. Then his lip tingled and went numb, and that night at the club, he laughed at somebody's joke and his face felt weird, like half of it was taped down. He ran to the men's room.

"Bell's Palsy," Chloe guessed.

"Right. You know somebody with it?"

"A friend, briefly. They gave her some steroids and something else, antibiotics? And it went away in like five weeks."

"Mine didn't." Ben had been saddled with a broken face for almost ten months. "So in the interest of not scaring anybody,

I taught myself this smirk. It used to go along with a shoulder raise and a little snort." He demonstrated. "I thought I'd appear clever and refined. They thought I was a stuck-up prick. I got blacklisted."

Chloe's brow furrowed. "Why didn't you just tell them the truth?"

"Embarrassed! Palsy? Everybody makes fun of the Palsy kid!"

The black behemoth under the chess table raised his head at Ben's outburst.

Ben leaned in and said in what sounded to him like a whisper, "That's the biggest goddamn German Shepherd I've ever seen. Or Doberman. I mix all those pointy dogs up. That's one of the few things I can say in Spanish. I can ask where the bathroom is, call somebody nasty names, and I can say the dog is big and black."

"We seem to have gotten off topic."

"Oh, yeah." Ben shrugged. "So I took up bartending. I'm a loser, baby."

Chloe sat back. "I'm to believe that a clever, successful guy—at least when he's not drunk—traveled three thousand miles, got himself on a stage, and then let a temporary embarrassing inconvenience kill his career?"

He struggled with her words for a moment, then asked, "What would you believe?"

"You wanted to be a bartender."

"Nice. Thanks very much."

"What's wrong with it? You make a lot of money. You're good at it."

"Who the hell are you to tell me what I'm good at? I was funny, goddammit!"

The dog looked up again, grumbled.

Chloe folded her arms. "Funny haha or funny peculiar?"

Ben smirked. "Very clever. Touché."

"I have another friend like you, he's this great teacher—"

"Please. Drop it."

"—but he scorns teaching and continues to struggle with his painfully mediocre—"

"Will you please! Shut—"

Two huge hands shoved him backward. No, not hands—paws. Ben's chair tipped, and a maw of white teeth snarled beneath smoldering brown eyes. He heard a sharp cry in a foreign language. He scrambled out of the chair, landed on his belly. Something dropped from his pocket.

The chess players circled him, he heard their bantering, saw their formal shoes. He noticed the one man's pants were two inches too short and that his socks were stark white.

Then he heard Chloe's voice rise above the chaos. "Hey! Where'd you get these?"

He squinted up at her, pinned by the weight of the dog who stood on his back and held gently but firmly to his neck, police dog style. She held a wallet. Not his. A worn, black wallet. And now she rubbed his nose in the funny orange money.

"These are pollution credits," she informed him. "Stolen from my company. You're in a lot of trouble, mister bartender."

"That's not m—"

A growl cut him off, made convincing by its teeth. He saw the minty green whirl of Chloe's dress and watched her platforms clomp out the door. A rivulet of drool ran down the side of his neck. At least it isn't blood, he thought. That'd come later, when the Porno Mafia people came after him for a wallet they knew he had.

Overhead, the distraught chess players flapped and squawked, and then Chloe's stereo rose above them with that same damn Duran Duran song. "Don't say a prayer for me now . . ."

It would not be denied. His lips pulled away from his teeth, and for the first time in years, Ben smiled. He smiled so big he thought he must be buzzing, like fluorescent lights or a muted television. You're in trouble! she'd said. He savored this. The understatement did it, pushed a hearty bark from the back of his throat: a laugh! Benjamin Myers, Bartender Extraordinaire, laughed and laughed and laughed.

The Snows of Jake Manjaro

It was all about the snow. Survival weighed in as a tight second.

If Blaze Benson had trusted his colleagues over the weathermen—had packed up and left before Stan's death, and the theft, and Jake retrieving that package—everything would be different now.

But there was "the snow." That's what Jake called and considered everything war journalists did. As in "snow job." And the media, the guys at the newspapers back home deciding what was worthy of printing, the guys who said when it was time to come home, they were the "weathermen." "Storm's a-brewing" Jake would say of a pending battle, and once the battle raged it became "a real hail storm." You'd've thought him a meteorology school drop out.

Blaze lit a fresh cigarette from the stub in his mouth, outted the stub against the well-worn table top. A habit he hoped he could quit once he returned home to the States. If he made it home. Had he left Chechnya with the others, he'd be safe now. But he couldn't. Because of the package.

Now he had to wait. Okay. A stint in prison had made Blaze good at waiting. Wait to go home or wait for death. He breathed a stream of smoke like a dragon. Prison and Chechnya, he thought, not so unalike. Both stank of fear and hatred. Except Chechnya in 1995 was "no kind of place to die."

Jake's warning, spoken the day Blaze had arrived. Diminutive Jake Manjaro seemed the Earthling of the future, with his British-Spanish accent, skin a nondescript shade of brown, eyes and hair (forever in his eyes, that hair) a few shades darker. He could have been from anywhere. He'd been just about everywhere. Blaze had covered three previous wars with Jake. Not partnered in a business sense, simply as comrades. In 1995, war reporters were still an orphic lot, likely to encounter each other at the most abstracted locales.

Blaze's first memory of his friend was from a muddy pit in Sokhumi. A small group of journalists, Blaze among them, had gotten caught in a spontaneous firefight between Georgian and the Abkhaz soldiers. High powered bullets ping-ping-THWACKed. Trees cracked open. Fist-sized clods of mud sprung up and people fell down, dead and dying. And there in the center of it stood Jake, camera hitched on his shoulder like a ghetto blaster, turning in an unhurried arc as if surveying for a new home. Daring death to come and fight him.

Jake's absurd machismo never spilled off the battlefield, though. Like frenzied snake handlers who succumb to epileptic seizures of divinity, in the bullet-thick of things Jake seemed owned by an entity outside himself. Back at "base"—the loaned room of a home, or a burned out basement, or on rare occasion a hotel—Jake spoke little and smiled often. He shared what he had, be it a piece of fruit, a spare battery, or a good joke. Only his opinions he kept to himself. He avoided drugs, drink, and the women who promised an hour of heaven.

Pragmatism kept him hard when he needed to be. Though seven years younger than Blaze's thirty-six, Jake seemed to have cut his teeth at war. Two years earlier, in Bosnia, he'd taught Blaze how to get through checkpoints, "borrow" motor vehicles, and sweet talk civilians out of food and liquor. He forged working relationships with warlords, snipers, and illegal arms dealers. Yet Chechnya spooked him.

From above the basement of the stone house the journalists had shared, Blaze could hear the whine of airplanes, underscored by thumping concussions of artillery fire. Like living near train tracks, Blaze now only noticed the ruckus when it went quiet, which was never, or when it was sliced in two by the screaming whistle of an incoming shell. That happened about thirty-thousand times a day.

Russia was throwing everything she had at this tiny country. Two weeks ago, all but Blaze, Jake, and Stan the Crazy Brit had left Chechnya's capital. The relentless shelling and ensuing horror rendered the other journalists paralyzed, unable to work, bags of jangled nerves. So they fled, lest they take on the hollow-eyed stare of the few remaining citizens of Grozny.

The Crazy Brit had been killed. A shell landed at his feet. Silently. Some of them do that. He'd been reduced to a pile of dogmeat, steaming in the crisp January air. Jake, unlucky, witnessed it, rushed back in a roar of adrenaline to pace and pant and share the horror with Blaze. Only Blaze had his own horror that day.

Blaze glanced now at the "package," a green backpack made neatly angular by its contents: Video and still footage, cameras and their film. Interviews with soldiers before the battles raged and after. Shots of abused civilians, misused corpses, and plenty of up-close-and-personal super-scary shots from the front. Plus three pocket notebooks filled with Jake's unsteady scrawl. Enough for a snow day. Enough for a blizzard!

The bag had been seized the same day the Crazy Brit was killed, perhaps the same moment. Taken from Blaze's vehicle at a checkpoint by troops or gangs, Blaze wasn't certain which and didn't feel it mattered. What mattered was the Kalashnikov at the base of his neck. How long had he been made to kneel in the mud? "Vrag naroda!" they spat at him, and he cried back, "Nyet, nyet, just a reporter." That icy muzzle digging into the flesh under his skull. They laughed and kicked him into the blood-soaked earth. Blaze sobbed silently, praying to a God he didn't believe in.

He'd told this to Jake, shaking and sick with shame. Jake, death-heady and filled with unprecedented belligerence by his friend's ordeal, had sworn to get the gear back. Miraculously, he'd done so. He burst into the candle-lit basement not three hours later, disheveled but un-bloodied, grinning like a fiend.

"Lookit! Lookit!" He held the bag up like the head of an evil prince.

Blaze nodded, embarrassed but pleased. He must have appeared recovered, since Jake lit into him like a drill sergeant. "Always carry cigarettes! Never let them see you're afraid! Never let them know it matters that you get where you are going, let them think you'd rather not be bothered, but that somebody is waiting, expects you."

Blaze mumbled that he knew.

"It's not enough just to know. You have to remember. When you're terrified and alone and think you might piss yourself. That's when you have to remember."

They shared tears and whiskey. The ground around them quaked; overhead shells shrieked. Teetotaler Jake had one quick shot then a longer one, then another. Apropos of nothing the calm man suddenly spat, "This is worse than Bosnia!" Blaze caught his friend's dark eyes and saw that hundred yard stare, dangerous in a journalist.

He'd only seen Jake flirt with hysteria once before, in aforementioned Bosnia. They'd followed a woman's keening to a barn, found unfathomable butchery. An entire village, een children, even pets. The keening woman, dying herself, held a slaughtered child in her arms. A true War Photograph, to be sure.

Jake had waded into the carnage. But he only clutched his camera, didn't raise it. A dozen steps in, his progress stopped. A sound came out of him, even eerier than the woman's as he shifted his weight from one foot to another in a small circle, breathing quick and shallow. Blaze had taken him by the elbow, led him out of the barn.

Bosnia had cracked something way down inside Jake Manjaro, and Chechnya was tearing that wound wide and ragged and bloody.

Deep into drinks after Jake returned with the package, a flicker of concern flitted through Blaze, burned off some of the liquor and left a branded impression. "Why'd you become a war correspondent?"

Jake gazed at him for what seemed like a long time, then seemed to make some kind of decision. "I was a science journalist," he said. "I believed that science is a unifying thing in our universe. A humanizing influence. As oppose to religion. Or war. But war is sexy, isn't it? Makes the front page? And I got to thinking, maybe there was something I wasn't seeing. Something I didn't understand. So I formed a hypothesis. And set out to test it."

"And?"

He waved an arm, indicating the war and all its madness. "Still in the lab." Then: "Wait for me. I'm going to find Anatoli and the Land Rover. We're getting the fuck out of here."

That was six days ago.

Blaze lit another cigarette. The dead stubs formed six neat rows on the table, each row a pack. I should save some, he thought, and then laughed out loud at his pathetic optimism.

A timid knock came at the house's heavy wooden door. Blaze squinted through the cigarette smoke. Not Jake. But probably not a soldier, either. He hoisted the package onto his shoulder, grabbed his parka and duffel.

Again, irresolute knocking. Blaze darted up the basement stairs and flung open the door.

Anatoli, the Russian driver Jake had gone in search of, stood in the doorway. Wide-eyed, bare-handed. Clutching a worn, gray wool trench coat to his neck. The biting cold left his endearing bulldog face ruddier than usual.

Blaze yanked him into the house. "Where's Jake?"

Anatoli looked at the floor, scratched his head. "He. Uh . . ."

Blaze nodded. "I figured."

"I can tell you: We are in not good place."

"Oh? How, especially?"

"Well, see, I can tell you: If we stay here in Grozny, we will most likely be killed. If we attempt to leave the city, on foot or by motorcar, we will most likely be killed."

Blaze blew an angry stream of smoke, pulled on his parka. "Die with your boots on, right? Do you have the Land Rover?"

Anatoli took a deep breath and said with patience, "I have yes. But is no driving in such whiteness I think." He splayed a hand, inviting Blaze to have a look outside. White flakes, the size of quarters and fast as bullets. A blizzard.

Blaze shrugged. "I used to drive for a living."

"Me, as well," Anatoli said quietly.

"I'm from Buffalo."

Anatoli paused, cocked his head like a curious animal. "I

have heard of this place." He yielded a jowly smile. "Okay."

Of course it was ridiculous. Anatoli was from Moscow. But, "Perhaps the weather will make the guards lazy," he said as Blaze started the Land Rover.

Moments later found them alternately praying and cursing their way along the icy, mud-filled trough passing for a road to Ingushetia. Behind them the sky throbbed orange and rockets streaked and screamed. Grozny burned. In front of them the trees lay flat, shrapnel and broken glass crunched underneath the tires, and the snow assaulted them like an angry boxer.

They traveled for over an hour before finding a roadblock. A checkpoint. Anatoli swallowed audibly. But Blaze reached in his shirt pocket, found his cigarettes. He took one, then offered the pack to the guard, who accepted. Anatoli made a comment in Russian about the weather. The guard said something about Vodka. Blaze offered him the whiskey, and it served as their passport.

"He tells us road is clear," Anatoli said as they pulled away. "No more soldiers. Only nature."

Russia would eventually be driven from Chechnya, resulting in a short-lived, unsuccessful period of self-rule. Gangs would take over.   Russia would be bombed and in 1999, Putin would swear to hunt down the insurgents in the toilet if that's what things demanded. Russian hostages would be taken at a theater and two years later at a school.

All this would begin the following year.

But at that moment, it was just Blaze and Anatoli. And for them, right then, it was all about the snow.

WINNER!

Howie Mead pulls the foil lid off the yogurt container and finds he's won! Closer inspection of the lid reveals to him just what he's won: A trip for four to Mexico.

Hmmm.

He rinses the foil circle and sets it on the counter, then roots around the breakroom for a spoon. Usually, like tonight, he can score a snack from one of the office refrigerators, but silverware is tougher to come by. He opens the seldom-used dishwasher. Dumb luck grants him a plastic fork, stuck down under the dish rack. He wrests the little white utensil free, leans back against the counter, and samples the yogurt.

Yuck! Tastes like chewable vitamin C. Musta belonged to one of the office ladies.

He takes another bite and examines the lid again. Does he want to go to Mexico? He doesn't like Mexican food. He doesn't like yogurt either, but the yogurt's free. Don't they tax you for these trips? Besides, his wife probably couldn't get the time off. Too many sick days already. Probably be good for her, though. Sunny and warm. And they've never had a vacation, not even a honeymoon.

But four people, who else would he bring? His brother-in-law speaks Spanish. But his folks would be pissed if they found out. Of course, her folks would be pissed if they found out about his folks.

Howie wrinkles his nose at the yogurt. It seems to get worse with each bite. Who would eat such awful stuff? Probably Carrie, that hag from HR. She speaks Spanish, too. Maybe she bought it hoping she'd win. And look, she did! Maybe he should tell her.

But geez was she mad last time, when he ate that banana she left overnight. If she wanted it so bad why didn't she take it home with her? The guys from dayshift told him she'd been in the kitchen kicking cupboards and slamming doors and hollering about What makes people think they're entitled to my lunch? Over a banana.

Naw, if he told Carrie he'd found a winning lid while eating her yogurt, she'd freak out. Write him up, or something. Could you get written up for eating leftover food?

"Evening, Howie. Whatcha munching on there?" Eddie displays a mouthful of crooked teeth.

"Yogurt."

"You a health nut now?"

"That's me. Gettin' healthy."

The lanky mechanic pours himself a cup of coffee. The last cup, Howie notes.

Eddie blows across the top of his mug. "The machine downstairs is full, you know. Snack guy came today." He slurps some coffee, peers at Howie over the top of his mug.

Eddie, Howie knows, has been to Mexico. For their honeymoon. Eddie's wife's not sick.

Howie eats another forkful of yogurt.

Eddie nods once. "See you at lunch."

"Dale ain't here today. Pedro is though."

Eddie shrugs. "So we'll play kings on corners. No poker. Later."

Howie scrutinizes the yogurt again. Damn stuff didn't even fill him. He checks his wallet but it's empty as usual. Maybe Pedro will loan him a couple bucks. Or maybe Pedro's wife made Howie something, sometimes she did that. Either way, he has to go to the downstairs breakroom, since that bastard Ed took the last of the coffee.

He retrieves the foil lid, folds it in half twice, holds it over the plastic yogurt cup. But he hesitates. He tosses the cup and fork into the garbage. The lid, though, he slides into his jeans pocket. And then, Howie Mead heads downstairs.

The Linguist Gets a Clear View

Today is my last lesson with my favorite student. Twelve years of teaching and I have never fallen for one of my pupils. Before now.

Perhaps it's my age. At thirty-eight, certain taboos no longer maintain their mysterious validity. A little life experience allows you to distinguish forbiddances of real ugliness from things which are merely impolite or inconvenient.

Perhaps it's the man himself. Fritz Sebastian Mueller is handsome, intelligent and funny. Businessmen are a dense lot, but this one is different, he's an engineer. The Germans believe that their salesmen should be technically astute. So his German-owned company shipped him here to the States, put him in sales and then sent him for private tutoring to reduce his accent. Sometimes I get lucky that way.

But today is his final day. We end. I neuter him, teach him how to pronounce those th's. With most of my students I love this day, this final lesson, this day of lingual castration. How can they not know what an advantage their little accents are? That Americans, unlike the rest of the world, adore a foreigner, will embrace and nurture him.

Well, let's be candid, will adore a European foreigner. French, German, Icelandic, Italian or ooh, British! accents have this wonderful advantage that employers fail to recognize, and fail to exploit. Instead, they ship all types of crooked English—twangs, drawls, brogues—to me for squelching.

And squelch them I do, wiping clean all traces.

It starts innocuously enough. We sit down and I have the client read. We make a tape. It's all downhill from there. I have him bring me a list of words he uses often and has trouble pronouncing. I then force him to read the list to me, repeatedly, at every session, over and over and over, while I correct him every time. I record him, I make him buy books on tape, and if he's really not getting it, I put my fingers in his mouth, "put your tongue here."

For this torture they pay me. Quite a bit, they pay me. It's a good job for people who would like to be dentists but don't like teeth.

Most of my students hate me in the end. They are thankful, thankful that they can pronounce thankful. But they hate me anyway.

Fritz is trying not to. Trying so hard that he asked me to lunch in the ninth of our fourteen one-hour sessions. "If I put food into your mouth, will you stop?"

I said yes. It was lunch, it was innocent.

He drove. The morning had presented drizzle and dingy skies. But at eleven thirty, those skies were parting, pulling back to reveal a deep blue. We stopped at a light and Fritz peered through the windshield, then pointed east.

"Look at zat! It is beautiful."

A rainbow. Where the gray clouds entangled blue sky, sunshine caught the mist at just the right angle, and a spectrum shone clear against the storm above.

A smile spread across my face, a big one. Here sat a man whose self-consciousness often drove him to speak in a near whisper, yet he unabashedly pointed out a rainbow and called it beautiful.

I thought about him after that lunch, and between our sessions. I thought about his intelligent green eyes and tousled brown hair, about his slender, tall frame and big hands. I felt a rush of warmth when I remembered him, and that same big smile would spread across my face. A crush! That's what it was. A thing I hadn't been plagued by since my undergrad days.

I enjoyed it, felt a gusto and zeal that I hadn't in a long time. Somehow when you're older, the crush doesn't seem the untamable monster you remember from high school. Instead, it grants the adult heart a curious freedom. Fond thoughts to put you to sleep at night, a compelling new reason to look forward to work. Something extra and superfluous, like the ribbon on a present. Yes, it is a strange longing this man has awoken in me. But not unpleasant, or wholly unfamiliar.

He is due here this morning, in twenty minutes. Usually, there is less of a lag between students, but both my nine and my ten o'clocks called in with illnesses, leaving me a blank morning. I've read the same sentence three times now. I'm too distracted for Jung, apparently, so I spin my chair around, lean my elbow on the marble window ledge, and gaze out the window.

Ten stories beneath me, the good people of Philadelphia scurry, their pace alone lending them purpose. They clutch their collars to their throats against the bluster of a sharp wind. I see through them, into the past, eight years ago, when I was living in Los Angeles.

I turned thirty that spring, and celebrated with a two-week voyage home, to visit my beloved Philly. When I returned again to California, I was elated. Giddy. First, because of my wonderful family whom I love, especially my Gramma who's my favorite person in the world. Second, because all my best and crazy friends lived in Philly, and I'd spent two weeks with them. And third, because of Joey.

"Look, this is Joey, short for Josiah, his parents are Amish and he builds houses for a living, isn't he a scream!" And all my L.A. friends obligingly screamed over the photos of the college-athlete-turned-construction-guy Joey. Joey who was conveniently working on the house next door to my parents the two weeks I was there, Joey who made me promise to look him up when I came back for the holidays.

I didn't show those pictures to Cody, my boyfriend of four years. A suspicious omission, I know. But Joey was three thousand miles away and of no true consequence. He was teeny-bopper, sleep-over fodder. We never hooked up; I gave him long hugs and thought about him sometimes in the bathtub.

Joey was relevant only in relation to the others. Yes, others. Before I'd gone on vacation, there was Zack. I found Zack on the Internet. No, not that way! I'd reconnected with him through that grad-pals.com. I'd known Zack since third grade. Third grade. Think about that. I know I did. It turned out that Zack had also wandered from the City of Brotherly Love. He lived, in fact, just over the hill, about twenty-five minutes from me. Like the other two guys who responded to my short, well-wishing, re-introductory letter, Zack was single.

I emailed Zack for six months, that's half a year, and somehow never found an appropriate time to mention that I had a boyfriend. Zack was always doing things, like feeding the homeless, or running AIDS marathons, or rescuing stranded sea lions. Intriguing stuff they make documentaries out of. We went to a few museums together, and Zack regularly pointed out his singleness. I bit my tongue. I never touched him either. The subject came up. I always told him that I'd known him too long, it would feel incestuous.

The thing about Cody, the boyfriend, is that we never clicked sexually. He's a composer and I'm a linguist so we had great intellectual intercourse. But that will only get a girl so far. Still, I was reluctant to forfeit the friendship. So I did the selfish thing and strung him along.

A lot of people—friends, relatives—argued that Cody and I were doomed anyway because of Scotty. I worked with Scotty, and he'd always intrigued me, if for no other reason than the fact of his height. He towered six feet, eight inches. How tall are you? He's got a foot on most people. And nicely built, and from money. Always traveling, all over and I continually wondered what that would be like, to take a trip with your beau and not have to pay his way. Because, in case the thought hasn't crossed your mind, there's not a whole hell of a lot of money in classical composition.

But Scotty only decided to be interested in me after I was already dating, and living with, Cody. We had lunch, Scotty and I. Lunches. I showed him the photos of Josiah. The less available I became, the more interested Scotty seemed. We had lunches right up until the week I moved from L.A.

Of course, there was also the chef. Jean-Yves. From Paris. He wore clogs and stood only as tall as me. He spoke English haltingly, and he was great in bed. Jean-Yves came before both Cody and Scott. But he drank and drank and drank, and I got tired of him creeping around my porch at all hours like a big Parisian tomcat. "What I want is: boy drives up in car with flowers, we go to dinner. What I get is you drunk at three a.m. with a hard-on."

That marked the end of us, but not of him. Jean-Yves had a great house in Studio City, south of the Boulevard and up in the hills. He had to go up North, to San Francisco, for a year, and he rented the place to me. (Cody moved in later.) Jean-Yves called me. Begged me to rent it from him. "Only in dis way can I know all will be safe. My house and its dings."

I couldn't have said no, not with the nothing he wanted for rent. Cody and I lived in that place for a year. That was the year I visited Philly, and Zack and I were planning our third museum visit, and Scotty was taking me to lunch twice a week, and of course Jean-Yves called once a month for the rent and that inevitably turned into a three-hour conversation.

One day I couldn't do it anymore. It was a day that followed a month of Cody nuzzling me for affection and me having headaches or cramps or something, always something. I finally decided I was being unfair and gave him the lecture. The one that starts with, "Don't interrupt me and don't change the subject," because anybody who knows the adult breakup process knows it takes a minimum of three times to get the other party to listen and actually pack their bags and leave. But I did it.

It was in the fall, like it is now, which doubtlessly contributed. Autumn has always been for me the season of new beginnings, not Spring. Perhaps the residue of so much schooling. I remember going onto the back porch. I had a bottle of fancy water and a clear view of the valley below; that wide, sprawling expanse of green. Green is a luxury in Southern California.

And I said to myself, "This house with this view could be mine. Along with matching quarters in San Francisco." I sipped my fizzy water.

"Alternatively, I could date Scotty and travel the world. See Europe, Thailand, Australia. With the same ease that I now get lunch from him twice a week."

I finished the water, and couldn't resist the urge to blow across the top of the bottle, forcing from it an eerie resonance.

"Or, I could date Zack and live an exhilarating, enviable life filled with intrigue and good deeds." Oh the possibilities!

The bottle was weighted for the cliff, as a flat stone is weighted for the water. I tossed it over the side of the porch, heaved it like a baseball and surveyed its decent—thunk, clunk, smash! And the moment it smashed, I started to giggle. I giggled and laughed, and laughed till I cried. Because, I realized, I didn't want any of them! I was glad to be free, just me, my messes, my money, my Sunday morning.

And now, eight years later, on this late morning, sitting here waiting for Fritz to come for his last session, I'm feeling like that again, only in contrapositive. I want Fritz. Clearly, plainly. I have a terrible crush on him, an affection and longing that remind me: I'm alive! It's exhilarating and wonderful.

I've dated since I moved back here. Are you kidding? It's been eight years, of course I've dated. Without the appetite and drama of my twenties. Spent time with people I felt no particular craving for, but who didn't annoy the hell out of me. Because as a person gets older, she realizes that these people are difficult to find. And you begin to think that maybe this is what it's all about, a soft fondness instead of a raging passion.

This revelation of mine disappointed me only slightly. I never fought and scratched and bit and seethed like my parents, and the dull comfort I'd found was preferable to that. If this pleasing ennui was the alternative to late nights of shrieking about money and housework, then I felt I should welcome it with open arms, and sip my brandy and shut up.

And then Fritz arrived. And now it's different.

For seven weeks, that's almost two months, we've held sessions twice a week. He's whined and complained at the exercises I've made him do, and he's yelled at me for humiliating him. I've yelled back for his laziness and hollow accusations. Once I told him to go to hell. When he left I figured I'd never see him again. That his company would call mine and I'd be fired the next day. They'd be right to, an instructor is supposed to keep her cool.

Instead, he showed up at his next allotted time, fully prepared with his rules and his lists of findings and difficult words.

" . . . and weird means strange. Which I can remember because it is spelled strangely." A grin. "In the case of double vowels, American puts the pronounced vowels first. Wheet, boht . . ."

"And?"

"And it's English, not American."

"Very good."

"Zank you."

I didn't apologize, and neither did he. Our mutual stubbornness hung as a lusty tension between us, which we enjoyed for the duration of two and a half sessions.

"I know what I'm supposed to do," he'd say.

"So do it."

"It is not my muhzer tongue. So, I am struggling. If I asked you to calculate zee required torque for an engine, could you do it?"

I admitted that I could not.

A session later we verged on another outburst, which Fritz curtailed with the offering of lunch. On the way there he pointed out the rainbow. At the restaurant, I asked him if he enjoyed sales.

He shrugged. "Is all right. So long as one is not selling pabulum, you know?"

"Did you like engineering?"

He shrugged again.

"My father was an engineer," I told him. "They made him a manager after so many years at the place, but he always longed

66

for the plant floor."

Fritz made a face. "Nostalgia for zee gutter, zat's what zee French call it. I don't miss it at all."

"So what do you like?"

He gazed at me, eyes sparkling. Then, a self-conscious smile and he changed the subject. "Why do you say ore-enge and people on the street say ah-range?"

I laughed at this. "Because you're in Philly! It's a colloquialism."

"I ain't liking it." He turned red. Then asked quietly, "Is zat right? Ain't liking?"

Now I really laughed. "No! Definitely not. I can't teach you that anyway, it's slang. Your boss would strangle us both!"

He laughed along with me and we ordered dessert.

Was that really only five weeks ago?

Even gazing idly out the window from ten stories, I recognize Fritz when he tumbles from the car. Recognize his neat clothing, his uneven, childlike gait. The wind rakes the last few stubborn leaves from the trees, kicks them through the streets. A short while later I hear his shuffle down the small hallway from reception, his shoes scuffing against the tile like a petulant teenager's.

He nods without looking at me when he enters, takes his traditional seat at the round table where we study. He wears a black V-neck sweater, charcoal T-shirt, black pants and black shoes. His normally forward-combed hair is pushed in all directions, an endearing mess. Much like his English. His dark clothes make him look older than his forty-three years. Sunshine glints through the window and describes deep lines in his face, evidence of a life filled with balanced joys and sorrows.

Fritz squirms in his seat, removes from a briefcase two tapes and a note book. Now he looks at me. His eyes are dark

67

today, forest instead of emerald, and his ruddy lips sneak into his traditional self-conscious smile. I return the smile.

And what will I do today? Place my index finger against the back of his teeth, just where the bone meets the flesh? When his tongue comes to meet it, draw the guiding finger away? And repeat it and repeat it until he can do it without the guide? So that when he says "that," it will be "that," and not "zat?"

Why, no.

No, I don't believe I will do this.

Fritz's crooked speech is the thing which united us. That made us yell and fight, that made him buy me lunch. Let some other cruel linguist wield that final knife, cut that perceived cancer from his speaking. I have a different idea, other plans for Fritz. For Fritz and my Sunday mornings.

Roadless Homelands

Arturo's voice comes through the squawk box like a watchdog, barking everybody to their destinations. Since I am already at mine, I turn the volume down so he's a distant growl. But not off. Never off. It's comforting to have that watchdog in the background.

Usually, by the time we get to the scene, the body is gone and the spectators along with it. But somebody new to LA Sheriff's keeps calling us immediately after he contacts the coroner. This past month, often as not, we beat the meat wagon.

This is one of those. The cops let me in this time, they don't always. They're not supposed to I don't work for the county. They just call us to clean up the stains—blood, puke, entrails— make the rooms or the highway look nice after the coroner's crew hauls the body and all the evidence is gathered.

But sometimes they let us into the scene and it can be interesting. Like this gig. It took a minute for my eyes to adjust; it's dim and cool in here. But now I can see the place. The living room is crimson, gold and hunter green, with exposed ceiling beams and antique maps on the walls. The cop at the door says the dead guy ran an Old World Antique shop from his house, but I've never seen furniture like this outside a museum. A desk like a Buick. Table bigger than my whole apartment! Who buys this stuff?

Even in death the guy had taste: He died on an overstuffed green-leather couch. Good of him to croak on the sofa, means almost no mess for us. They must have found him quick, too, because that pungent/acrid smell isn't around yet, just a raw meat scent and the metallic tang of blood, like maybe somebody was slicing up a roast. Mostly we'll be cleaning up after the detectives on this one, finger print powder and Luminol. Though at the moment, they are doing more arguing than detecting.

"I call bullshit on that, when's the last burglar you see carry a rifle?"

"He was shot?" I ask before I think.

Her laser eyes find me. "Yeah. Somebody popped him through the chest with a thirty-ought six. Looks like he was napping at the time."

She notices my company patch—the Grim Reaper with a broom instead of a scythe. Below that is my name tag. "Makes your job a little easier I guess . . . Fabienne?"

I nod.

"Is that French?"

"Haitian.

"Same thing."

"Not to the Haitians."

The lady cop takes in my gray eyes, caramel skin and wiry chestnut braid, tries to fit these into the equation I've just handed her. It's higher math: I was born in Haiti to my anthropologist father and the mulatto woman he stayed with—an intimate form of imperialism. I spoke only French and Creole until I was five and we moved to the States, "back" to New Orleans: I saw "home" for the first time as a Kindergartener.

Still, me and this detective, we've got a lot in common; there aren't many women here in the land of the dead. Dealing with the deceased, especially when the cause of death is violent, requires a certain temperament. Every coroner and mortician and most homicide detectives I've met, they all display a detached philanthropy, a sort of sympathy for an equal but different species. It's a lonely compassion. Maybe most women are better at feeling like a part of the human race.

The detective and I stare each other down for a long moment. After looking me over good and hard, she doesn't quite smile. "How come you're here so early?"

"They called me, I came. How long you think till he coroner gets here?"

"They say five minutes and it takes them fifty. Why don't you go buy yourself a coffee?"

I can take a hint. Or, in this case, a swift kick in the ass. I head outside. The sky is an impossible blue with just a few fluffy clouds so perfect they look fake. Los Angeles in spring. This is what people flock here for, how they envision it is all the time.

The neighbors are clustered in groups on the dead man's lawn, projecting the usual sound bytes to the police: Sob, sob, sob, " . . . such a nice man."

Aren't they all? Once they're dead anyway. All so nice. No one ever says he was a son-of-a-bitch who deserved it.

The police officer sounds bored. "Did you see anyone suspicious?"

"Hard to know. As an antique dealer, he had a large number of people coming and going all the time." The neighbor crosses his arms and strokes his chin, as if deep in thought. "Could have been a stranger or a customer who wanted something, could have been anyone."

He actually says this. Could have been anyone. I don't know how the cops do it.

I'm amazed at how calm and resolute the neighbors are, though. I figured a murder up here would shake this place up better than an earthquake. This is Valencia, LA's newest vestige of Great White Flight. It's all green up here, big lawns and oak trees, like you're in some east coast town and not the middle of the desert. In October, even with temperatures still in the 80's, the trees obligingly change color and drop their leaves, albeit reluctantly, like kids whose bedtimes comes before it's dark out.

I call Arturo to tell him I'm on a Zombie. That's what he's taken to calling it when the van goes out too soon, Zombies. I guess because the corpse still has to move.

At first I thought he was making fun of me because my mama runs a shop selling Vodou stuff to the tourists in New Orleans. Most of it's bunk—she never practiced Vodou, at least not that she'll admit. But she gives the Yankee visitors a trashy side show, because that's what they want and it pays the bills.

The money and everything has all been her responsibility since I was 12, when Dad left New Orleans for Chicago. He wanted to take us, but Mama couldn't bear it. New Orleans offered something of her homeland, even if only an echo. Anyway, turned out Arturo didn't even know I was Haitian, he thought I was Hispanic. Which annoyed me, even though a lot of people make that mistake.

Arturo doesn't answer; I get his voice mail with his sing-songy Mexican accent that I like, find soothing. I leave him a message, then lean up against the van and eavesdrop some more. To hear the neighbors tell it, Jean Rene' LaSalle was the perfect neighbor, everybody loved him. So why is dude lying face down in a puddle of his own blood? No signs of forced entry, no evidence of a burglary . . . And what's a single guy doing in a bedroom community like this? Bet he was quiet.

Sometimes I think I'd like to be a cop. I like puzzles and appreciate a challenge. But I come from a culture wary of police. Besides, Mama was unhappy enough when I told her about this job. You know, Haitians have an odd relationship with death. We sort of admire and fear and mock it all at the same time. New Orleans, too, has weird relations with the Gede—the Spirits of the Dead. That's what happens when you either bury your dead above ground or have them float away in the next good storm, you laugh even as you're crossing yourself.

This job didn't make sense to my mama. It seemed like hateful work to her. And I can't completely argue. I wouldn't say you have to despise people to do it but it probably helps. I'm not talking a dissatisfied, *I've had nothing but lousy boyfriends* kind of hate either. I mean a deep seated *Daddy tried to kick me to death in the womb and I survived just to spite him* kind of hatred. The kind where you walk around with a permanent snarl and laugh at cripples.

That's not me. That's our boss, that's Arturo. That's why he looks forty when he's only a few years past my 26. But it makes him strong, too, it's why he never flinches. Not me. My first decomp, I threw up. All over my new uniform. Then I started crying because it was this old guy whose wife had died and he couldn't stand to be alone so he'd shot himself and that made me sadder than anything I'd ever heard. A crying, vomiting girl—just what Arturo wants to deal with. I thought for sure I was fired. But nope, he sprayed me off with Versitol, said finish the job, go home, get drunk and come back the next day if I wanted. I did. Haven't thrown up since.

A tug on my jacket pulls me back to now. I don't look like a cop, but I look like something official in my navy blue uniform, so people often ask me questions. I turn and look down and find little girl, maybe nine years old, with white-blonde pigtails and a red T-shirt and jacket.

"My sister wants to know where's Belle?" she implores. She pronounces belle in correct French.

I squat to be at her eye level. Clutching Red's hand is a younger child, also a girl, with a ponytail down her back. Her dark hair makes her skin look the color of a porcelain doll's. Her shirt is green and has a monkey on it. Cute. I ask, "What's wrong?"

"Belle. She's missing."

"Who's Belle?"

"Jean Rene's dog."

The younger girl tugs at her sister's jacket and gestures with her hands, looking like she's trying to keep hold of a parakeet. Sign language! Red nods and tells me, "Belle was long and short and she's gone."

Long and short. "Is Belle a Dachshund?"

She stars at me blankly.

"A wiener dog?"

Now she gestures to Monkey, who responds in turn.

"No," Red tells me. "She's a crime dog. A Basket Hound."

"Oh, a Basset Hound, huh? And she's missing?"

"I don't know. Did you find her?"

Suddenly, I'm an idiot.

I take the girl's tiny shoulder in my hand. "We will do our best. Please tell your sister."

Whose kids are these? I look around but no one seems in close enough proximity to be responsible for them. I crouch back down, ask Red where her parents are.

"Mom's at work," she tells me. "When Tommie forgets to pick us up, Jean and Belle watch us."

"Watch you? Like, your babysitter?"

She nods.

"Who's Tommie?"

"Her Dad." Red points an accusing finger at her little sister.

"Do you have any other relatives? Gramma? Or an aunt?"

"Gramma Mary. She lives at 1016 . . . uhm . . . Winston Street! In New York."

This gets better by the second.

As you might guess, Children in Peril is not a topic that wrenches my heart strings. Still, these kids make me admire them. They seem tough. I lead them to the side of the van and make them promise to stay there while I seek out the detectives.

By now the coroner is here, along with the press, so inside the house it's madness. The cop guarding the door shakes his head at me. I consider asking him to tell the Detectives about these kids. But even from the driveway I can hear the police arguing with the coroner's Deputy about moving the body, and the Deputy bitching at the news people. I guess they've got enough to worry about.

The kids are still at the van. "Hey, you kids want some Meat Klown burgers?"

All kids love Meat Klown . . . I herd them into the van, drive up Newhall Road and drop twelve bucks, getting them some Kiddie Klown meals. While we're sitting in the noisy orange and yellow restaurant eating, Monkey notices my necklace, it must have come out of my shirt. It's a purplish, crooked heart, made from metal clay.

Monkey wipes her hands on her napkin then points to the heart. I hand it to her so she can look at it. She reads the engraved French, "Ce qui est nécessité secrète et restera ainsi." Her brow creases and she shows the heart to her sister, forgetting I'm still attached to it, and yanking me forward.

Red wriggles her nose. "Something about a secret."

"What is secret must and shall remain so," I translate.

"Who taught you French? Jean?"

Red nods. "Who bought you your necklace? Your boyfriend?"

I smile, shake my head. "My mama."

I run a finger over the cool metal of Mama's farewell gift to me. I left New Orleans the minute I graduated high school, have lived in seven American cities since and found work in every one. Waitress, bartender, telemarketer, data entry, retail, lab tech, denier . . .

I could never explain why I needed to go. All those cities I've lived in, every one aroused in me the strange, removed feeling of a person who knows a place but can never truly be part of it. It's a sad and crippling longing, and it began in New Orleans. I was afraid Mama would be angry or deeply saddened. But she said I had to go where my heart led me, and gave me a necklace to keep me safe and remind me who I am, where I come from.

Monkey nods in approval at the shiny trinket. Red signs something to her, and says to me, "Lizzy likes your necklace."

"Oh? Tell her thank you."

"I like your hair."

"Thank you, too, then."

"Yeah, because it's like a big thick rope. We could swing on it!" She falls into shrieky giggles. I laugh along with her; I never thought of it that way, but she's right. My hair is thick and frizzy, but not nappy. It takes work, but I wind it all into a thick French braid that runs to my hips, like a rope.

As we're finishing our fries my phone rings—Arturo: "Where the hell are you?"

"Meat Klown."

"What the hell ya doing there? Get me a Bozo Burger. And get over here! I've already snapped the photos, it's time to hustle." The little beep tells me he's hung up.

Him barking like that means everyone's cleared out; I missed the detective and need to go to work. "What time does your mom usually get home?"

"Around ten. But sometimes she has to work a double. She's a nurse."

"Where does she work?"

"At the hop-spital."

"The hospital here? In Valencia?"

The girl's big blue eyes search the ceiling. "Uhm. Yeah? No, maybe not."

*　*　*

Arturo's enormous black pick-up sits alone in the dead man's driveway. "SHTKIKR," his vanity plate says. The coroner's van, cop cars, and media wagons have split to the next scene, the next story. The neighbors have crept back inside to phone their friends, brag about their tragedy and "Did you see me on TV?"

Arturo comes sauntering out of the house as I pull up. He swaggers like a Carnival dancer, shoulders high, chest back, dick leading the way. He's one of those blond Mexicans, el Diablo Blanco, with storm-blue eyes and a permanent five o'clock shadow. Arturo is pretty goddamn sexy, which is good because if he were an ugly man, there's no way he could get away with treating people the way he does.

He struts to the van, confined in a protective blue paper suit. It includes booties, but for smaller jobs he cuts them off, revealing his black steel-toed work boots. His gasmask rests around his stubbly chin and the hood of the suit drapes back over his broad shoulders. I hand him the yellow bag with his food. "You owe me six bucks."

"Yeah? I'll take it out of your check for being late. Get

suited up." He reaches into the bag and starts back inside, but only makes it to the stairs. "No ketchup!"

He scowls up at me from the porch, and that's when he sees inside the van, sees the kids. The yellow bag drops to the doorstep and Arturo comes back, swearing. The kids shriek; Arturo frightens a lot of people. His power comes through despite his modest size, like a pit bull.

He smacks the side of the van with his fist and the girls screech again. "No riders!"

"The detective gave them to me," I lie.

His eyes narrow.

"Their mom won't be home before ten. The dead guy is their babysitter."

"¡No digas mamadas!" He pounds the van with his fist again. "The detective would have interviewed them and turned them over to Child Protection. Don't lie to me about my own job!"

I swallow and stare at the lawn.

He runs a hand through his tawny hair, gazes at me in a way that could mean he's sorry. "You can't have them in the van. It's not legal. Find a neighbor who'll watch them. I'm gonna eat. Then we'll do this, then we'll call the cops or something. Chingalo! I don't have time for this!"

I pick the most exemplary house in the cul-de-sac: An SUV and a minivan. Plus a barking dog, and a collection of plastic toys and bicycles littering the lawn.

I head up the walk, but a voice tells me, "You're wasting your time."

I peer around the Minivan for the source of this wisdom, and discover a maybe-college-aged kid with spikey dyed black hair, skull wristbands, and skater sneakers. He munches microwaved popcorn from the bag.

"You live here?" I ask

"Unfortunately." He gives me the once-over. "Want some popcorn?"

I take a handful. "I'm Fabienne."

"I'm Bryce. And I'll tell you right now, nobody in this cul-de-sac will help you with those kids."

"That's mighty white of 'em."

He tries not to grin. "Their mom? Her boyfriend or baby daddy or whatever—"

"Tommie?"

"Yeah. He rides this loud-ass Harley and comes home at two-thirty in the morning like, all the time. Wakes the whole neighborhood up. They don't like that, this is the suburbs." He offers me more popcorn. "Plus, I think they're all jealous," he says.

"Jealous?"

"Yeah. All the moms are in love with Jean Rene, but she's the only one who's single and could maybe hook up with him. You know, 'cause her and Tommie are on-again-off-again. And nobody seems to see through him, how shady he is."

"Tommie?"

He shakes his spikey head. "Jean, I mean."

"They pretty much say he was perfect."

Bryce yaps a laugh. "He's not even French or anything! His real name is John Rene Gonzalez. Gonzalez! That's about as generic as you can get."

"In Los Angeles, anyway."

He frowns slightly, like he's unsure what I mean, like he's never heard that the rest of the world exists. "He made up this fancy name and speaks a foreign language so all the women adore him. Girls are stupid."

It's my turn to frown—there are uglier reasons for changing

your name.

Bryce raises both hands, thinking he's insulted me. "No offense!" Then, "I kind of know where Terrie works," he offers hurriedly.

"Terrie?"

"Miss Kneal. Danielle and Elizabeth's mom? Lizzy and Danny Girl, she calls them."

I don't tell him I've been calling them Red and Monkey. I also don't say anything about the gleam in his eye when he talks about Terrie Kneal. Maybe that's why the moms don't like her.

"The kids already told me she works at the hospital. But they don't know which one.'"

He grins all crooked, like he's trying not to. "Hospital? Not exactly!" He laughs despite himself. "I don't know the name of the place? But I know it's down near Miracle Mile. Off of it, near the Peterson Museum, you know? Next to the Cajun-Creole place."

This piques my interest. "What Creole place?"

"I don't know the name of that either. But they make some killer jerked fish. It's just one room with about ten tables and nothing separating you from the kitchen."

"Why do you know all this?"

"Sometimes when Terrie's car isn't working I give her a lift."

I'll bet you do.

Both our mouths are full of popcorn when I see Arturo strutting his way to us. "What's going on?" he barks from the middle of the street. "You find someone to watch those mongrels?"

"Not yet."

His glare finds Bryce. "You can't watch some kids for a couple hours?"

"My stepmonster won't let them in the house."

"So watch them at their place," Arturo snaps.

"I don't got a key, man!" Bryce rises, steps away, tosses his shoulders back.

But his hostility is no match for Arturo. "Key? So what! Break a window! Climb through it and let them in the door. Then watch TV for a few hours till Mom gets home."

"Dude. I can't break into somebody's house."

"It's their goddamn house!"

The boy cringes. I wipe popcorn grease on my pants, step between Arturo and Bryce, say to my boss, "You're bitching that it's illegal to keep them in the van, now you want us to break into somebody's house?"

"THEY LIVE THERE!"

Bryce scurries to the safety of his own home. I suppress my instinct to shove Arturo's shoulder.

"Nice going, tough guy. He knows where Mom is."

"Didn't he tell you?"

"Only sort of. And it's an area I don't know."

Arturo swears in two languages and stomps in a circle. "Fine. Fine! Leave them in the goddamn van until we finish this job. It's a small job, no floor boards need to be torn out or nothing, so shouldn't take more than a couple hours."

He heads back across the street. I follow him, feeling like an abandoned sidekick. "We can't leave those kids in a van by themselves for four hours! Call Frank, tell him to take the job over. You're gonna need him anyway to spackle over that bullet hole."

He turns, shoves a finger in my face. "Do you run this company?"

"Come on, Arturo. Just drive me down there, huh? We'll drop the kids off and I'll buy you dinner at the Creole place."

"We just ate."

"Sure but it'll take us time to get there and stuff."

He leans against the side of the van, gazes inside at the two little girls who, amazingly, are still preoccupied with the crappy plastic toys from Meat Klown. The juxtaposition of Arturo and children is odd; there's no room for anything so normal in his life. Arturo works any and every minute that he doesn't sleep. The company runs 24-7, and if he could find a way, he would too. I've often wondered what he's hiding from.

I've gotten hints; sometimes he'll take me for drinks after a particularly nasty case. He'll have a few and mumble oblique regrets. He has a sister here, I know, but the rest of his family is still in Mexico. He served in the Mexican Army, knows guns, and carries a concealed weapon. I know he killed a man, not while in the military, but beyond that I don't know the circumstances. I know his father is dead, but not why or how or for how long.

I'm quiet for what feels like a long time, watching him watch the kids. He scowls, looks at them more closely, then looks to me again. To my surprise, his eyes soften and his mouth forms a hesitant smile. "You'll buy me dinner? Buy me some Voodoo food?"

"Stop with that crap. Before I give you the evil eye!"

His shoulders shake with quiet laughter. "Alright, Fabs. I'll call Frank. But we have to work until he gets here."

I agree. I dig my gear out of the back of the van and explain to the kids that they have to sit tight for another half hour. I made them use the Meat Klown bathroom because I didn't want them in the crime house, so I figure they'll be fine.

In the house, Arturo is blasting his mariachi music. I appreciate it, it's so upbeat compared to our job. Together, we wrap the blood drenched sofa in red HazMat bags and haul it outside, toss it into the back of Arturo's pick-up. Back inside,

I check for blood on and under the carpet, while he scrubs the Luminol, which seems to be everywhere.

"They sure made a mess of this place," he complains.

One thing I can't escape, the core of this job, the cleaning, always seems to spark pity in me. Yeah, the kids should be with their mom, but there's a dead guy that they might be able to help.

"Maybe we shouldn't drive down to LA," I say. "Maybe we should just drop the kids off with the police. You said they'd be taken care of, right? And that way their memories are still fresh."

"They're just a couple of kids. Nobody cares what they have to say. And they didn't see nothing anyway."

"How do you know?"

He shrugs. "They ate, right? They're not traumatized."

I don't know jack about kids. Arturo at least has nephews. "But the dog is missing. The girls told me that."

"So?"

"Seems to me if you find the dog, you solve the case."

"You want to solve crimes or clean them up, huh? I lose people this way, don't think you'd be the first. Go! See what I care." He pauses and inspects whatever he's cleaning, rubs a thumb against his fingers. "What is this?"

I take a look. It's a coarse, off-white powder, all but lost in the oatmeal-colored carpet.

"It's like polenta," he says.

"Polenta?"

"Cornmeal."

"Think it's important? Like a clue?"

Arturo shrugs. "Cops signed the release." Once his hand-held vacuum is silent again he says, "Don't they use cornmeal in that creepy religion of yours?"

"It's not my religion, so I don't know what you're talking about."

"Yeah, they do! They draw those symbols on the floor for the spirits to come through, what are they called?"

Veve, they're called and the thought of such a beacon at a murder site chills me. But I refuse him the satisfaction. "Monsieur Jean Rene was probably making French tortillas. Corn crepes!"

There's a knock at the door, then Frank appears, a dark-haired ox in a Tyvek suit that matches ours. His haunted blue eyes catch mine and he nods once in greeting.

Frank and Arturo go back about twelve years, when Arturo drove the meat wagon for the coroner's office and Frank was an EMT. I guess after jobs like that, cleaning up debris isn't such a big deal. Frank never threw up on his shift, I know that.

Arturo tells him where we are and Frank takes over wordlessly. Outside, Arturo and I strip out of our blue suits and bag them, along with the gloves. "We'll take the van," he tells me, and he claims the driver's seat.

We take the 5 South to the 405, through the Valley and into the city. Arturo knows right where Miracle Mile is, the wide, clean stretch of Fairfax that's edged with museums. Their modern edifices stand out bright against the dingy side-streets littered with burned out, for-sale-or-lease box structures, streets that channel into regal Fairfax like streams to a river. We pass the Museum of Modern Art, The LaBrea Tar Pits, and just off Fairfax, the Peterson Auto Museum that Bryce mentioned. We drive up and down a handful of roads, then a pale blue and yellow building catches my eye, and sure enough that's the place.

The allegedly Creole restaurant is called Mama Jama's. For Crissake! Arturo just about drives the van through the front window, he's laughing so hard. Next door to it is Zulu's. Animal skins cover the windows, and a three-position neon leg blinks over the door, its warm glow just visible in the dimming evening light.

Arturo sits back in the driver's seat, makes himself comfortable. "Go find Mom."

"Me? You're going to miss an opportunity like this?" I flip a thumb at the neon leg.

Arturo squinches his nose, makes a sound like he might spit.

"Alright." I hop out of the van.

Inside, six men in suits are dispersed at four tables around the stage. Most of them are watching the basketball game on the TV behind the bar. A faux leopard carpet covers the floor, its cleanliness telling. The bar is made of bamboo, and different fuzzy animal patterns cushion the matching barstools. All very shiny and upscale.

The music matches the décor—upbeat and rhythmic with a lot of drumming. The dancer is dressed like Tarzan's girlfriend. Then she spins around the pole and whoosh, she's suddenly in a leopard thong and pasties.

Having grown up in French Quarter, naked dancing girls are nothing new. Still, I always find myself envying these women, who are so unapologetic, so comfortable with their bodies. I watch her writhe and shake her creamy self and it moves me, you know, gets me going a little. Not for the lady, but I discover I'm wishing Arturo were here.

This stuns me. I'm the only chick on his payroll (except for Marguerite in dispatch, but she has grandchildren in high school). Arturo and I once had a candid discussion about this, and the possibility of hooking up. "First," he told me in his alcohol-worsened accent, "Don't get your meat where you get your brrr-ead. And second, I don't want no kids, so I don't have no sex." I figure he was jiving me on that second part. Still, I took his rejection at face value and never allowed myself to think of him that way.

I bite my lip and step to the bar, where a white girl with blonde cornrows rifles through a bartender's bible. I raise my voice over the music, tell her who I'm looking for. Her lips purse slightly. She sets her hands against the bar, the band of gold on her left ring finger striking the ivory top challengingly. "That's me."

She catches my quizzical look, glances at her ring. "Keeps the men away," she explains. "Some of them, a little. Anyway, who are you?"

"I'm, ah . . . you're babysitter's been killed."

An odd expression flits across her face. "They catch the guy?"

"No clues."

"So what is it you need from me?"

"I've got your girls," I tell her, sort of surprised that she hasn't asked. When a sharp V forms in her forehead, I hurriedly give details.

"Oh," she says, "Jean Rene' is dead," like it's just sinking in. Then an exhausted sigh: "Oh god, Tommie."

She again sighs visibly, glances at her cellphone. Then she looks me over for along moment, like the detective, like the teenager. Finally, "I can be off shift in an hour."

"I can keep them outside till then," I offer. "I mean, I drove them all the way down here, right? I'm, you know, trustable."

She smiles and nods. Offers me some money that I turn down. I trot outside feeling relieved. From the van comes a noise like a box full of frightened gerbils. I toss the passenger door open. "What's going on in here?"

Monkey—Elizabeth—points to the alleyway between Zulu's and the Creole place, makes a whiney noise from the back of her throat which her sister imitates.

Arturo takes Danielle onto his lap. "See that cemetery-

86

looking gate? The girls are telling me the dog is back there."

"The dead guy's dog?"

"Yeah."

"So go check it out," I tell him.

"You go check it out."

"I went into the strip club!"

"They're your people."

"What?"

He gestures to the ominous black gate. "Go take a look. There's a whole neighborhood of 'em. Creepy-ass Voodoo dudes." He averts his eyes and sort of shudders.

"You're scared."

"I look like a Gringo!"

I don't know whether to laugh or be insulted. "They won't eat you."

I step around to the front of the van, to see if I can catch a glimpse of the dog. Elizabeth bolts from the vehicle, runs off through the iron gate. "Hey!" I jog after her, snatch her hand and yank her to me. "Don't run off . . . like . . . ." Ten yards and the world has changed completely.

From the restaurant comes the scent of frying pork fat, along with the characteristic smell of frying green peppers, onions and celery: "The Holy Trinity" of Louisiana Cajun/Creole cooking. Chickens run through the passageway between the two buildings, a wide alley lined by low porches. Hidden here between and behind the businesses are tiny, cheap apartments. The apartments are less Louisiana and more Haiti.

The entranceways have all been painted stunning colors—flaming orange, deep green, sea blue. Many of them have drawings of serpents or hearts, or murals, mostly of saints. A Rada drum—cone shaped and four feet high—leans against the porch closest to us. The porches are not enclosed but many of them have been covered in vibrant fabrics, brassy patterns splashed against bright backgrounds.

It's like wandering into a dream, familiar yet distant. I was so young when we left Haiti, sometimes it feels as if I never really lived there, only constructed a world based on Mama's stories of the place. But some memories are undeniable as snapshots, so vivid and visceral, and this hidden neighborhood has made them tangible, in concrete and cloth and Creole. The place rings with the language, in songs and murmurs: sophisticated French brightened by the tonal rhythms of West African tongues.

Elizabeth breaks free from me, easy in my stunned state, and races to the second porch, where a gray-haired, dark skinned man rocks slowly in a creaky, bright red rocking chair. He turns toward the girl and I see his eyes are milky, though he seems to look directly at her. His face remains neutral. He calmly pets the animal in his lap, a well-fed, drooling Basset Hound.

Seated on the step next to the rocking man is a young guy, his glaring face dark as polished ebony. The younger man pulls himself to his feet, aided by a walking stick. His shadow is long and skinny in the late day sun. He wears loose cloth pants tied with a piece of rope, a red and black shirt, and a wide-brimmed straw hat. Elizabeth sort of skids to a halt.

She waves at the young man and points to the dog, then points to herself.

The young man smiles slightly, perplexed.

Elizabeth jumps in place, makes her howly noise and points to the dog, then herself, then the dog again. The Basset Hound's head lifts, and her ears perk forward. She squirms as if to stand. The old man strokes her, says be still, hound, it's okay in Mama's language.

Though I still understand it, I no longer speak it, and I'm dredging my memory for the words I need to communicate—

Chien an se . . .—as the young man's grimace returns. And suddenly I notice that it's not a walking stick he's leaning on, it's a gun. I don't know a hell of a lot about guns, but I do know that a thirty-ought six, which killed Jean Rene, is a big rifle, and that's what this man's propped against.

Arturo materializes at the gate. There's ferocity in his saunter and menace in his glare. He clutches a tire iron. One hand rests on the small of his back, on his pistol. His eyes flit from the rifle to its owner, to the dog, to the little girl.

"We're fine," I whisper through clenched teeth.

But he keeps moving toward us, toward me and the girl. I scramble in front of him. Set my hands on his shoulders, shove him backward, hissing. "Get back in the van!"

His eyes widen. But he stops.

I scoop Elizabeth into my arms and, shaking my head at the young Haitian, say the first thing I think of in French. "Non chien de langue française." We're not looking for a French-speaking dog.

I charge back through the gates, hustling Arturo in front of me.

His stormy eyes pierce mine. "¿Que chingados?"

"They killed him," I mumble. "And he deserved it."

Once we're on the other side of the gates, I set Elizabeth free. She scuttles into the van and the two girls sign frantically at each other.

"The Haitians killed Jean Rene'," I tell Arturo breathlessly, "and they took the dog as payment or something. Probably she gave them some money, too. My guess is he was maybe touching them."

He gapes at me. "For that, for your guesses, you get to yell at me? Shove me around!" He glares at me for a long moment. Then his whole demeanor changes. He laughs. He laughs! Right

89

at me and I want to punch him in the face.

"You don't know shit about shit," he taunts.

"You're so smart, you tell me why they killed him!"

"I don't know!" Arturo throws open his arms. "You don't know either. But nobody who talks like your mom can do something bad, huh? "

"What?"

"You think because they talk the same language and eat the same food that you ate growing up, that they're your kin. That you're like them. More like them than you are like Jean Rene', or like those kids. Or me. I can tell you: You're wrong."

He is telling me this from experience. His own—dark and ugly. I know the depth in this statement, and I know the truth of it too, and it stings. So I sidestep it. "What does that have to do with the dead babysitter?"

"Those girls loved Jean Rene. He wasn't doing nothing bad. Tommie's the one they're afraid of."

I consider this. I think about Terrie's confusion, almost like she'd been expecting someone to be dead, but not Jean Rene. Maybe Tommie. Maybe the Haitians, they got the wrong guy. Or what if Tommie hired them to kill Jean Rene? Didn't Bryce say everybody thought Jean and Terrie had a thing going on?

Arturo quells all this. "You're missing the point. For all we know, those men killed Jean Pierre—"

"Jean Rene'."

"Whoever. They speak French, he speaks French—"

"They speak Creole."

"—this whole thing might have nothing to do with anyone except all those French speaking pendejos."

"Creole. They may or may not speak French."

Again, he waves me away, laughing.

Again, it pisses me off. "So what, now you want to go run

to the cops? Tell them we found the dog and turn those guys in?"

"I never said nothing like that." He pauses. "Just, you should care less about making these violent men blameless. They are nothing to you."

He leans in. "Or is this going to be your excuse now to move from here? To leave Los Angeles, like you left everyplace else."

I glare at him.

He rolls his eyes. "Where now? Brooklyn? Haiti?" His fist catches my chest. "Live where you live. Be where you are."

"Whadda you care!"

Arturo laughs again. "It costs a lot to train you guys." But the hardness is missing from both his voice and eyes. Even his smile softens. "Mija, there is no road to take you home." He says this with a sadness. "El Corazon es una tierra sin caminos."

I'm too stunned by his use of a term of affection to ask right away what the Spanish phrase means. I recognize heart and road . . . a land without roads. . .the heart—then giggling from the van disrupts us, muddles the moment.

Arturo curses mildly in Spanish. "Guess they've recovered."

"Just why were you willing to come down here? Why didn't you just dump the kids at the station house before?"

He shrugs, tries to stay nonchalant but I can feel him toughening back up. "Before we started cleaning the house, they were talking in the van, remember? They were late getting to Jean Rene's today. Stopped to chase a kitten on the way home or some shit. Anyway, they were convinced it was their fault."

I must look horrified, because Arturo puts both hands up. "I talked with them, they know it's not. They understand now."

"Okay. Good! But I still don't—"

"I don't want nobody's kids around the police!" He says this with such force that I flinch. His nostrils flare with a few sharp breaths, but when he speaks again his voice is calm and low.

"Things can go wrong with kids and cops."

"Like?"

"Foster care. Court. What if they wanted those little girls to testify?"

I'm mulling this over when something occurs to me. "How did you talk to them?"

"The older one talks."

"But you said you heard them. In the van."

"I didn't say I heard them," he mumbles.

I gaze at him pointedly.

His hands move, and he speaks precisely. "I. Can. Sign."

I gape at him.

He waves me away yet again. "One of my nephews. Here in the States."

I stare at Arturo, perplexed. First because I had no idea. But too, because he's telling me not to throw my lot in with random strangers who speak my language, while he's defending these kids.

He reads this accusation in my face.

"It's different," he tells me. Not an argument, simple information.

And he's right, it is. Despite the alarm in me, signaling me it's time to move on, find my roots, my people, my home. The men I am trying to identify with took a life, then called upon a sprit to consecrate that act. A spirit I know of but do not exactly believe in. Just as I once spoke their language but no longer do, as I recognize the smells from the restaurant kitchen, of foods I grew up eating but do not prepare for myself.

Then there is Arturo, the Devil I Know. His anger, his kindness, and the dark fuel that drives him, a potion I have caught the scent of but never tasted. I rub my chest where he tapped me, feel the coolness of Mama's metal heart. What is secret must and shall remain so.

There are things never meant to come to light. But too, there are things that need to walk in the sun. And what path shall we take? The heart is a road-less land.

Evening has settled on Los Angeles, streaking the sky red and purple, and leaving the streets deep blue. Arturo leans up against the van, next to our company logo. In the shadows, the Grim Reaper's cowl and broom make it look like Arturo is sporting a top hat and carrying a cane.

"You still owe me dinner," he says.

"Maybe we could get Italian. I saw a place on the way."

"Maybe we should get Mexican." He winks at me.

Perhaps it's the place I've just been to, but the vision of him with the hat and cane makes me remember Gede Nimbo, the spirit of the dead, also regarded as a special protector of children. I smile in the dim light, thinking that even where there are no roads, a compass still points north.

I lean forward and kiss his cheek. "You're a real gem, Arturo."

He sighs, but slips an arm around my shoulders. "Thanks," he tells me. "But I'd rather stay stone."

Tango in Wasteland

The first time I heard Club Graceland called Club Wasteland, it came slurring out of my very own mouth as I sat around a beer-sticky table of divorced single-moms just like myself. None of us realized how old thirty-eight was until we hit it. "I feel irrelevant," Trisha would say, then finish her gin and tonic. Sandy would nod. "I don't know what matters anymore."

Loneliness and co-misery drove us each down there in separate vehicles every Thursday night to drink, listen to the amateur DJ, and most of all watch Leon.

A glance at Leon led one to surmise there'd been some inbreeding, that his eventual wedding cake would be made from Twinkies, that he owned a deer's ass doorbell. But Leon possessed the kindness of angels and the hips of a slumming Adonis.

He moved along the tiny dance floor with heartbreaking grace, his western button-down shirts and golfer-plaid pants belying his toned, tan, mid-twenties body. "Dance with me, Mama" he'd coax, grinning gap-toothed. "Are you too good to dance with me?"

One at a time, he'd request our hands and we'd offer them up, Yes. He'd slip his college-age arm around our late-thirties waists and for a few minutes, the duration of a song, we'd feel like the queens we had all once been. Against the four-four time of three chord progression, Leon taught us the Cuban Rhumba's basic box steps, bestowed on us the Italian Tarantella's inherent mercurial adoration, even spoiled us with the twists and dips requisite of the Argentine Tango.

Leon hummed while he danced and when he didn't dance he talked. "I'm going away," he promised. "I'm going out West." He never said just what for. His friends thought him ugly. No one believed him. Nobody ever left, and if they did they came right back before year's end, full of excuses and fingers pointed in all directions except center. We nodded and smiled.

One Thursday, the DJ arrived and played record after record, and no Leon. He'd gone West we surmised, stunned. Done just what he said he was going to. Once he'd been gone a while we began to wonder if we'd invented him, participated in some group hallucination to stave the static sadness.

Leon hasn't come back yet and I don't believe he will, though no one has spotted him on a soap opera, or sit-com, or Dancing with the Stars. But it's been more than a year. No one dances at Club Wasteland anymore.

Yes, This is a Fine Promotion

Ed jutted a thick, blunt finger, rapped its tip against the subway car window.

"What the hell is a whistle-pig?" he asked. The finger stayed pressed against the thick plastic.

Adam followed its aim between the bobbing heads of other morning commuters moving on and off the train. Through the smear of the El window, he found a new platform vendor with an incorrectly apostrophed sign:

Whistle-Pig's! (World-Famous)

"Sausage?" Adam ventured.

"Hotdogs I'll bet."

"At this hour?"

"This is Chicago." Ed splayed his hands in an exaggerated shrug, bringing up the hem of his pinstriped suit. "So long as there's no ketchup on 'em."

Adam peered at the bright, hand-lettered sign, yellow on blue like the sun against sky. "Watch my stuff—I'll find out!" He ducked off the train into the farty, diesel reek of the station, the orange-cast lighting dim and unpromising after the garish fluorescent of the subway car. In his pocket, he located change from the twenty he'd broken at Emerald City, the coffee shop by Sheridan where he caught the redline in the morning.

Adam seldom bought coffee and he'd never—never-ever!—left the train mid-route. But he felt sprightly this day, one of those late February days when the sun cracks through the grayness, encouraging people to stroll open-coated despite no significant temperature change.

Apparently a lot of people were feeling sprightly, as evidenced by the animated line leading to the whistle-pig cart. The now-penultimate guy was about eleven feet tall and would have eclipsed the very sun from Adam, had they been topside. The blonde in front of that guy had murdered a Muppet—giant, fuzzy, purple—to stay warm in the winter months, and currently obscured Adam's horizontal sight-line with her questionable fashion sense.

"In PA," some stranger Adam could not see attested, "a whistle pig's a woodchuck."

"What's a woodchuck?"

"A groundhog!"

A hot wind pressed from the far tunnel, foretelling the arrival of the outbound. The stranger raised his voice over the bluster and the accompanying ominous, mechanical rattle.

"Damn, man, I ain't trying to eat no Punxsutawney Phil! Shee-it, I thought it was sausage.

Despite his protests, the man didn't move from the line.

Adam glanced at his wrist, which bore no watch, then back into the train car. His nonchalance began to recede, shooed off by commonplace anxieties. His cellphone, laptop, even his morning coffee all waited on the train while he stood in this slow-ass line. And what were they all waiting for exactly anyway?

Across the platform, the outbound squealed and grinded to

a halt, a robotic voice aboard announcing the stop, which looked only slightly different from all the other stops, Adam supposed. Would he recognize it if he got off at the wrong place one day? The Lake stop, where he exited for work, had been re-lamped a couple years back, thereby recognizable by its bright, greenish cast. But several of the points South were also being re-lamped. And even trudging up the stairwells into the city might not clue him in, since all of that looked about the same as well.

He took another sticky step forward, noticing the same stark anti-smoking ads he knew were displayed where he boarded, but here, Blue Cross Healthcare and Are You Pregnant? hung alongside them. Lake didn't exhibit those; theatre show placards hung in their stead. Adam knew these things, intellectually, but the more he tried to envision the Lake platform, the more indistinct it grew in his memory, forged instead in his mind by images of the platform he stood on now, just as the music one is listening to obscures a song one is attempting to recall.

All this made him unhappy, and concerned again about the time. He remembered that his wallet was still in his coat pocket, from his rush at the coffee shop. The thought of all his things together without him incongruously soothed him. Like having a pet you knew would greet you at your door upon your arrival home.

A man at the front of the line moved away grinning like he'd won money. But a white, wax bag kept his prize a mystery. Adam tried to see into the little cart, but the Tree and the Muppet killer kept the whistle-pig a secret. Whatever it was smelled good, not like a hotdog, but some kind of rich, flavorful meat. What would he put on it? Would it be on a bun? Or ooohh a biscuit! Maybe it would have gravy, it kind of smelled like there was gr—-

DING DING DING

Shit!

Adam lunged for the car closest, two away from his own, managed to get onto it before the door swooshed shut. He squeezed past a dark, glaring woman who cursed him quietly and a gaggle of teenagers who stepped around him like they would a stray dog. Their clutch of noise and motion made it easy for him to slip unnoticed through the arched door to the next car. He excused-and-pardoned his way the length of that car as well, past young women with shiny black hair talking loud and fast in Spanish, and dull sleepy men, and people of indeterminate age bobbing heads to music, squinting at newspapers or cellphones. He nearly tripped over the stripy-stockinged legs of a girl watching a movie on her cellphone. He caught himself on the back of a seat, garnering no reaction from its occupant—a drowsy boy in a Penn State sweatshirt reading a Japanese comic book. Behind him, stripy legs still intruded the aisle.

Finally he found the door to his car, just as the train slid to a stop—making him feel stupid for not just waiting until it stopped in the first place to get back to his car. But this, Adam knew, was Ed's stop, and he could see the neat man there at the far end, perusing the car, glancing at Adam's things, his brow folded in indecision. Adam hollered the man's name and the brow unfolded; Ed waved a disproportionately large hand in farewell and stepped off the train to begin his work day.

Moving forward through the exchanging populace proved simpler than when he was the only one in motion, but it seemed to take longer now that Adam knew his items were defenseless. He returned to his previously-shared red and orange seat, rendered unmistakable by the smiley-face-and-crossbones graffiti gracing its back.

Adam's things waited there, his laptop and briefcase, his coat with his wallet in its pocket, and even his morning coffee, all still right where he left them. The problem was that a man wore

Adam's coat. Wore Adam's coat while one hand clutched Adam's briefcase. Read a newspaper Adam had inherited. And sipped Adam's coffee for Chrissake!

Flummoxation made Adam again behave uncharacteristically. "Who the hell are you?"

"I'm Adam Hellerman," replied the slightly stocky blond.

"No, you're not."

"Yes I am."

"No you're not!"

"Who am I then?"

"That's what I'd like to know!"

The man shoved a business card at Adam—one of his own. Adam Hellerman, it proclaimed, Dealer-to-Vendor Relations.

"That's my card."

"No it's not."

"Yes it—"

"If it's your card, why do I have it?"

"Because you have all my stuff!"

"All your stuff?"

"Yes!"

"Including your empty wallet and your secondhand trench coat and your bitter morning coffee."

"Um—"

"And your newspaper."

"That's not my newspaper."

The man raised Adam's coffee in a one-armed shrug. "Well here, you can have it."

"The rest of it's mine."

"Really."

"Yes!"

"For Chrissake, who in their right mind will believe you?"

"People steal shit all the time. Women steal babies out of

other women!"

"Okay. But who's going to believe that somebody was stupid enough to leave all their stuff unattended on a subway car?"

"It wasn't—"

"Along with an already stolen newspaper, Chrissakes!"

"Please stop saying that," Adam demanded.

"I'm sorry. Are you religious?"

"No. I say that." Adam ran a hand over his face. What to do? Nobody around wanted to notice. Would anyone believe him that he was himself and this man was somebody else? They were about the same height, but where Adam's build reflected the gymnast he'd been in college, the man claiming to be Adam presented like an ex-boxer. Adam's brown hair glowed red in the sun, while his companion's blended light and dark into a dimensioned two-tone once known as "dirty blond." Passable? If this man claimed Adam's photo ID as his own, would he be believed?

Adam examined the man's face: squarish, proportioned, generic. Much like his own, Adam supposed. He wondered: Would he spot himself in a group photo if no one informed him he appeared there? Would he see this man photographed among a group and mistake this man as himself? Adam himself had no ID to counter with, no sanctioned, authoritative laminated card or pamphlet proof to demonstrate that this man with all his stuff wasn't him, wasn't in fact Adam Hellerman, Dealer-to—oh!

"If you're me, tell me what dealer-to-vendor relations are."

The man's lips pursed slightly. Adam waved the business card, which the man snatched. And read while Adam loomed over him triumphantly.

"Honestly, I can't tell you," the man admitted.

"Ha! I knew—"

"All I do is sit at a computer all day and field phone calls from angry guys at big box stores who want to know where their shipments of valu-pak hambuger patties and extra-strength floor cleaner are."

"My god, you are me."

The man unsuccessfully suppressed a smirk as the train squealed to a halt and its cargo exchanged itself. "Care to sit?"

"I'd love to sit." Adam dropped into the seat beside himself.

"Got time for a story?"

"I think I have all day."

"It won't take that long. There was this guy, about six years ago. And he left New York and he came to Chicago. He didn't tell anybody he was leaving, and he didn't notify anyone when he arrived. He just left, and then was there. Here. In Chicago."

The man claiming to be Adam scratched his chin. He pushed a hand through his hair, succeeded in rumpling it.

"Why?' Adam asked the man, who grew scruffier by the moment. "Why'd he leave? Bad marriage or something?"

"Nope. That's the weird part. He had a pretty wife who adored him and a kid he dug—a daughter, a tomboy already at age three—and a mid-sized mutt that got along with the wife's fat tomcat. They all shared a breezy apartment in a decent part of Brooklyn. A sufferable twenty-minute commute from his boring but decent-paying office job, shared with people whose company he generally enjoyed. He played poker every other Friday, hosted parties year-round, which were attended by a broad intersection of upcoming artists and professional people."

"So why'd he leave?"

"That is why."

"You're losing me."

"It was lost on him, too. He had all the trappings, right? But nothing took him over. He felt complacent, not content. Not truly satisfied."

"No . . . passion?"

Adam's doppelganger nodded. "Exactly! Wow. What a luxury to be understood."

"Let's not get crazy, now. I mean, I can understand the motives but not the actions."

"What would you have done?"

"I don't know, find a hobby?"

"Like?"

"Coin collecting?"

The blond man's face slackened.

"Woodworking? Sky diving! Photography." Adam shrugged in surrender. "Not run away!"

"He didn't run away, he ran to."

"To Chicago."

"Right."

Adam's eyes hooded. "And what did he find there? Here."

"Well, that's the weird part."

"The second weird part."

"I think for most of us it's all pretty weird. Don't you think? It only seems familiar? Because we don't pay attention."

The dirty blond gazed at the subway window for a long moment, staring at the dark blur of concrete tunnel, or his own reflection, or maybe through all of that and into the past. Or maybe the future.

Adam cleared his throat unnecessarily.

"Hmm?"

"You were telling me what the man found in Chicago," Adam reminded him.

"Yeah. He found . . . well he found a pretty girl with a nice smile. And a German Shepherd that she liked to walk along the beach and that got along fine with the man's grey tuxedo cat. He found the cat the night he got off the train here. He and the girl never did get married, but they did share a big sunny apartment, and they did have a kid, a boy who didn't speak until he was three but whose first words were a complete sentence."

"What'd he say?"

"'It can't be done.' He was right, it couldn't. This boy liked to take things apart. He was smart like his mother, who taught organic chemistry at the community college. The two of them—the man and his girlfriend—played board games with three other couples once a month, and they hosted parties with her university crowd and his office mates."

The train lurched to a halt again: Automated voice and the optimistic bustle of Midwesterners experiencing that first sip of spring.

"If you're going to work," Adam told his companion, "the next stop is mine."

"So, why'd you do it?"

"Do what?"

"Leave like that. Like this."

Adam frowned. "No, I . . . it . . . I wasn't leaving."

"You'd already left."

"Not for good. Not on purpose."

The dirty blond slumped a bit. "Oh. Well how would I know that, really? When I saw your stuff there, all your stuff, you know. I thought you'd done what I did. Just walked away from it all. And I figured maybe you had something more . . . interesting."

"Like?"

"A torridly bad marriage where the police come."

"I'm single. Sorry."

"An embezzlement scandal to be embroiled in?"

"Not really. I've stolen some highlighters and those sticky arrows? You know the ones?"

"A play you've written? Or a novel?"

Adam shook his head with a sad smile.

"My god, I really am you." The blond scratched his stubbly neck for a long moment. "So. Why did you abandon all your stuff?"

Adam thought about this. For what felt like a long time, he thought about it.

The train slowed.

"I got off to get a whistle-pig," he finally declared.

The new Adam Hellerman stood. "What's a whistle-pig?"

Adam squinted slightly. "I still don't know," he admitted.

"Well. Now you can find out." With a wave and a bright smile, Adam Hellerman's coat and briefcase and bitter coffee and empty wallet all exited the train car.

Adam interlaced his fingers, folded his hands behind his head. He gazed over the heads of bustling commuters. Once the doors closed, he stretched his legs out.

"Now I can find out," he said to no one in particular.

But he suspected—deep-enough down inside himself that he could, for now, ignore and even dismiss as cynical skepticism the feeling, but he suspected—that he never would.

The train car rattled and rocked on the rails. Adam, inside it, smiled and swayed.

Berlin's Porter in New Orleans

They all want to know what she thinks. Of their hair, of their work, of their city. Of them. And of course, Berlin adores them. Berlin adores everyone.

Porter, Berlin's brother, just watches. He stands in the living room of his, and their, apartment, separated by space alone from the dining area where they all sit at the oval table, slurping oysters and jambalaya and swigging champagne. The bright apartment smells like rich food, like good living, like decadence. Its ten-foot ceilings make Porter look small.

As small as he feels. Small and amazed. Jealous? Perhaps a bit. Yes, most definitely a bit jealous, but not of her, not jealous of his sister, but rather of them. Berlin's kiss goes everywhere, but never seems to find him.

"Porter!" They holler, "What are you thankful for?"

He shakes his head to clear it. "What? That's tomorrow."

"Then wish for something! Maybe it will come true."

"I wish it would rain."

"You know, for a playwright, you're sure pragmatic." "Yeah, and a real bummer sometimes, too." "You should have a drink."

"Maybe a couple."

He mumbles something about needing the rain, but lets them fill a tall, slender glass with champagne, takes a long swallow, grins.

"He's always like this when he's writing." "Oh, no! Usually he's worse." "The fact that he's out here with us can only mean one thing." "He's stuck."

Berlin sidles up next to him, refills his gold-rimed flute from a bottle she's appropriated. "Are you stuck, Porter? Has your play become work?"

To Porter, Berlin is a raver Betty Boop. Her spit-curled hair shimmers with glitter, as do her lips, her eyelashes and her fingernails. In the sunlight, her hair glows violet, making her cat eyes sparkle emerald. She seems to him like a cartoon, walked off the screen.

"Stuck? No. But if I don't leave soon, I'm going to be late. If you're coming with me, you'd better get ready."

"What's to get? Do I not look ready to you?"

You look like you were born ready, he thinks.

He says: "I didn't know if you were still going."

"Why would I not be going? I said I'm going, I'm going. Are you, like, all right?"

Porter finishes his champagne, tosses the fancy glass into the fake fireplace where it smashes gratifyingly. "I'll get my coat."

He exits left, accompanied by his roommates' gleeful hollering. "Impressive!" "That's the Thanksgiving spirit!" "Thought you'd lost your verve!" "Didn't know you had it in you!"

When he'd first informed his roommates that his sister would be visiting, they were happy about it simply because they enjoy guests.

"What's she do?" they asked.

"She's a photographer."

"Like, for a living?"

"Yes."

"Wow!" "That's tuff!" "That's cool!" "What's she photograph?"

Porter chewed his lip. "Construction."

"Construction?" "And her name is Sharpe, like yours?" "No way!" They lunged for the oversized book, a relic from the previous tenants now kept on the mantle with the other coffee table books. Photo Construction Project 88, it's called. It's a step-by-step photographic documentary of the creation of 88 Wood Street in London, an "invitingly futuristic" skyscraper carried out in elegant concrete and glass curtaining.

"Berlin Sharpe is your sister!" "Didn't she do that flip book?" "The one where you can see the building being built if you flip it one way . . ." "Right, front to back." "And demolished if you flip if back to front!"

Porter nodded, silent, not telling them that the flip book, an enormous commercial success, had been her thesis project. Or that she'd photographed the construction of the sexy, famous Campo Volantin Footbridge, in Spain, where she'd lived on and off for the seven years it took to build.

"Berlin and Porter," they prodded. "A city of gates and walls . . . " "And the keeper of these things!" "Do you have a sister named Key?" "A brother Labyrinth?" "Labyrinth Sharpe?" "Sounds like a cheese." "Or a dastardly character in a play!" "There you go Porter, use that in the next one." "A photographer and a playwright. A lot of talent under one name." "And soon, under one roof!" "Here's to us!"

Porter could not and cannot compete with their vibrancy. They appreciate him, selected him as a roommate because he is quiet. To them, he poses a challenge. They've never asked themselves why he selected them.

New Orleans in November is chilly, so Porter drapes a scarf around his neck and a leather trench coat over his shoulders. The leather's musky warm scent grounds him, lends him confidence. He strolls through the apartment's tall French doors without hailing his sister. Moments later, her clump-clumping down the three dark, spiraling stories of wide wooden stairs brings a rush of satisfaction.

At the bottom of the stairs, Porter gazes through the locked, cemetery-style gate at the garden, shadowy in the evening. "That was lush and green just six weeks ago," he tells Berlin. "Now it's dried up."

His sister shrugs. "You don't have access to it anyway."

"It smelled good. Made it nice to come home."

They move through the lower foyer, through another heavy, wooden double door, and out onto the street.

Cabaret Dante, where Porter is a playwright/waiter, offers a 30s style burlesque show every night at midnight. Sometimes plays run during the week, otherwise bands take the evening stage. At seven, when Porter and Berlin arrive, a harmonica player squeals and howls around a rock-steady bass, while a washboard keeps time. The bar greets them to the right of the entrance, but Berlin glides the short distance toward the front.

Two rows of small round tables flank the low stage, with larger tables farther out and booths to the side of the stage. The smell of cigarettes is foreign to her, something she has forgotten, coming from California where it is illegal now to smoke in bars. It makes her feel like a wayward adolescent again.

Half of the tables are already filled. Berlin snags one in the very first row, watches the band, bums a clove cigarette from another patron. She lights it from the candle. Candles set in dark red globes sit on each table, providing the only light in the room besides the stage and the bar.

Porter appears in his white shirt and bow tie. "Show doesn't start till midnight," he shouts into her ear. He sets the Gin Fizz she'd requested on a black napkin.

"I know. I want to get a sense of where you work. Besides, your roommates told me the drinks here are cheap and strong."

"I think they were talking about the women. But whatever makes you happy."

Berlin plucks the cherry from her drink, takes a swallow from the wide straw. She snags Porter's sleeve, pulling him back into hearing range. "Who's the bassist?"

Porter glances at the stage. A buff white guy with neat, chin-length dreadlocks and a worn white tank-top works the bass, bobbing his head to keep time.

"I don't know who he is, but I'll tell you what he is: Smelly!"

Berlin laughs in a way that suggests to Porter she is slipping from tipsy.

"How can you possibly know that?"

"Because he was in the office earlier collecting the band's wages, and the whole damn office stank. Reeked."

"Like what? Patchouli or something?"

"No, like body odor. Like him! He smells bad."

Somebody's misfortune leads Porter to holler this as the song ends. The entire room becomes privy to his opinion, and anyone sitting in view of Berlin can follow her gaze and know who Porter is talking about.

Berlin smirks, shoves a loose fist at Porter. "Speak into the microphone, please."

A different waiter comes after that, tall and dark with some kind of accent. Berlin and Porter don't see each other again until just before midnight. "It's slow and Gregor needs the cash, so I'm splitting. You want to stay and watch the show?"

Berlin nods vigorously.

"I can come back for you afterwards if you want."

"No need."

"You sure? You still have to walk back."

"Honey. I live in L.A."

"All right." Porter leaves.

He walks the grid of cracked and crooked sidewalks through the French Quarter—north, west, north—to the Morgue. The Morgue warrants its name, and heritage, for the days of cholera and carpet baggers when it housed the city's dead. The bar comprises the same square footage as Cabaret Dante, but the Morgue's dim blue lights and open-faced front make the place cool and broadcast. Not a place to hide.

Porter asks for a double of Laugavalin, straight up. Ronan comes from the men's room, pulling his long hair into a smooth ponytail. Despite Goth being almost cliché in New Orleans, Porter appreciates the man's velvet tailcoat and black fingernails, finds his knee-length boots and ruffled shirt fitting.

Ronan orders them shots of pricey bourbon, toasts the night. "To Thanksgiving Eve, 2002. May it present us something good."

"Good liquor with a good friend."

The bourbon heats Porter's chest, making him feel lighter. "How's the ghost tour business?" He asks Ronan.

"Always good on the holidays. Fewer drunks. And the Cabaret?"

"Girls in lingerie. Can't complain."

"Where's your sister?"

"Speaking of girls in lingerie?"

Ronan's smile widens.

"She's over at the show."

"Does she like New Orleans?"

"She likes everyplace. New Orleans likes her, that's for sure. The roommates love her. I told you they practically drooled on themselves when they figured out who she is?"

"You'd think they'd have asked sooner. Sharpe not being a common surname."

Porter shrugs. "Maybe they did, and I wasn't listening. I got a big lecture this morning about how I'm not learning anything being here, I'm not listening to my roommates or my characters or the city."

"Wow. I hope she at least purchased the morning meal to lecture you over."

"Yeah, she took me to Madeline's. Berlin already knows more about New Orleans than I do. She's like that. Everyplace she goes is like home to her."

Ronan raises a pierced eyebrow.

"Perhaps she hasn't found her home yet." He hails the bartender for another bourbon. "She makes a wonderful tourist, though. Sort of a Matrix-meets-Audrey-Hepburn thing she's got, huh? Like she owns the place but seldom comes."

"My terminally cool sister." Porter orders another Laugavalin.

At fifteen minutes before two a.m., Porter leaves the Morgue, making it to the front door of Cabaret Dante just as the first patrons leave. He slips past them and hangs by the bar, waiting for Berlin. But he doesn't see her in the thin crowd. He asks Gregor, who says he served her drinks until 1:30, when she paid her tab. He doesn't know if she left or not. Neither does Tyrone, the bartender, or either of the barbacks. But the ladies in the show, they've seen her.

"That's your sister? Boy, is she funneee!" "A real pistol!" "You oughtta put that girl on a stage!" "We tried'da convince her ta do the show wid' us." "Yeah, but she says she's leaving this weekend."

"Do you know where she is? Where she went?"

None of them do. So Porter makes his way back home. He figures she slipped out the stage door on purpose, to make him worry, and gets pissed about it. Then he feels bad for being pissed, thinks maybe she won't be at home, maybe something awful happened and he'll never see her again and here he is being pissed at her . . . .

The house still smells of hospitality. The front room is empty. Only the kitchen light is on, but shrill laughter comes from the back of the apartment. He follows its source to his own bedroom, where all his roommates have converged. A step-ladder sits atop his unmade bed. The girls hold it steady while one of the guys is visible only to the waist, the rest of him consumed by the gaping maw of the dark crawl space above Porter's bed.

"Porter's home!" "Oh?" "You'll love this!" "Look what we found in the attic."

They cluster on his bed and hold up a stuffed raccoon. Taxidermied. The animal looks to have weighed close to forty pounds in life. Now, it stands on its hunches and clutches a teacup.

"There's three of them!" "One has the teapot." "A teapot!" "And is pouring!"

They fall into riotous laughter.

Porter jams his hands in his pockets. "Is Berlin here?"

"Wasn't she with you?" "You lost your sister?" "Already?" "She probably ran into somebody who recognized her."

He nods, telling them he's going to make a sandwich. "Then I'd like to go to bed."

In the kitchen, the dishes have not been done, nor has anyone handled the garbage, and all the spoiling food emits its greasy stench. Porter snags half a loaf of white bread, the peanut butter and jelly. He takes them to the denim living room couch, where he makes and eats three sandwiches, and drinks all the milk, right out of the carton. His achy head and queasy stomach remind him he should drink some water, but he's too tired to get up.

Finally, he goes to his room, from which his roommates have cleared. They've replaced the painted board leading to the crawlspace and taken the raccoon family elsewhere. So Porter supposes he has nothing to complain about.

He can't sleep. He feels guilty for being in his own bed; Berlin has been sleeping in his room. But she's not here, and he's tired, and his roommates are still up, chatting and laughing. When she comes back, he can always move back out to the couch. If she comes back.

A rush of fear courses through him—he prickles with sudden heat. He takes a deep breath. He should get up and look for her! But she could be so many places. Maybe he should work on his play. But he knows he wouldn't be able to concentrate on it. Dammit! He rides the pendulum again, anger, fear, anger . . . but those double-shots of whiskey finally do him in and he dozes off.

* * *

"We're going to the store." "I'm not, I'm going with her." "I'll stay here and make some coffee, help you bring up the stuff when you come back."

Just as it lulled him to sleep, the chatter of his roommates greets him in the morning. He creeps out of bed, pulls on sweatpants, and opens the French doors to his balcony, letting in damp, chilly air and the white-washed morning's deceptive brightness. A horse clip-clops its way down his street, hauling a buggy with two early-bird tourists and an animated guide.

His spider plant, perched on a milk crate, has grown brown and sad. Looking at it leaves him low. He pulls in a long breath, lets it out in a loud stream.

"You alright, Porter?" Alexis steps to the adjoined balcony from the room she shares with Devlin. She lights a cigarette and then makes a sound matching Porter's.

"Fine. Just waking up." He squints at her. She reminds him of a music box ballerina, graceful but limited. "Did you do something to your hair?"

Alexis straightens up. "Yeah. Your sister suggested it. I was going to color it fire-engine red but she said no, use a henna wash. I'm glad." She smiles. "I like it a lot. Cheaper, too."

He squints at her some more. Notices her very deep blue eyes and freckles. He nods. "It's flattering."

In the kitchen, Porter finds the dishes washed, drying in the rack. The room is clean, its foul scent replaced by that of freshly brewed coffee. Devlin's down comforter lays rumpled and forgotten on the living room couch, and a blend of sweet honeysuckle and sensual amber oil lingers like a ghost. So Berlin has been there, slept, awoke, and left again. Without waking him.

He pours himself a cup of coffee, happy to find it kissed with the peat-and-tannin tang of chicory. He craves buttery, sugary beignets but is afraid to leave the house. When will Berlin be back?

Loud voices echo from the staircase, and moments later, the guys tumble through the door. They swarm the kitchen, squirming their way around Porter, dropping overflowing grocery bags and snatching pots and pans from the lower cupboards.

Porter steps to the dining area. "What are you doing?"

"Starting the turkey, man." "We wanna eat by one." "That means no stuffing!" "I guess. Think that's cool with everyone?"

Porter shakes his head, lauging with disbelief. "I've lived

here four months and never seen either of you make anything more complicated than a bowl of cereal."

"We didn't want them,"—Devlin juts a thumb to the living room to indicate the girls—"to know we could cook." He winks at Porter, who suddenly realizes that all Devlin's clothes are the same olive green, and how he's always crinkling his nose, like it itches. "But your sister totally busted us."

Kirk nods. "Got us to braggin'," he drawls. And Porter remembers; Kirk is from Texas.

"So then we had to prove it."

"Where is Berlin?"

"Buyin' a table."

"We have a table."

"For the foyer," Alexis' voice rings from the living room. She curls her feet under her on the sofa's matching arm chair.

Porter closes his eyes. "You got a cigarette?"

"Since when do you smoke?"

"Since they cook."

Porter retreats to his balcony, where he lights the cigarette. He again considers revising his play, but the thought makes him tired. He knows it reads badly; does not know how to fix it. Can't find an ending that works.

His hand stings. Burned. Porter curses, drops the spent cigarette, watches it fall three floors to the broken sidewalk below. He considers going down after it—no littering and all—but it hasn't fallen near anything flammable.

And what if it had, anyway? What if the whole damn house went up in flames? Might take this torturous play away from him. Might give him something to write about.

He steals a clean towel from Devlin's room and heads to the shower.

A short while later, the noise of his sister's return overrides the spray of water, even the rattle of the crippled fan. Porter finishes quickly, steps to the wide, cold marble floor and dries himself. The shower is separate from the toilets and lies in the exact center of the apartment, so he senses as soon as he exits the shower stall that everyone has left. He stands enveloped in the warm steam of the large room and listens.

Rowdy laughter spills from the foyer, carried along with the sweet scent of beignets. This generosity follows him down the chilly hallway, wafts all the way back to his room, where he yanks on a pair of black jeans and a dark blue sweater.

He follows the laughter to the spacious foyer, not quite full even with all four of his housemates and Berlin. "Look!" Candice shrieks, pointing. The stuffed raccoons from the night before are having a tea party. They sit on barstool-high chairs flanking a round, steel table. The wrought iron of the bistro set is curled into elaborate, mercurial swirls that animate the furniture—it might walk away on its own in the middle of the night.

"A steal at the French market," his sister tells him. "And I got some old French Cabaret posters. And the boys are going to cook us Thanksgiving dinner!"

Behind her, lugging the fourth chair up the winding staircase, comes a buff young white guy with dreadlocks. The bassist. He's got a flannel shirt on over the ubiquitous tank top. Once he's positioned the final chair, he gazes at the floor and chews his lip. Berlin drapes a black-lace-clad arm over his bare shoulders. "This is Ezekiel."

"Zeke," the musician says quietly.

"Since he was kind enough to agree to help me with the furniture, I've invited him for dinner."

"Awesome!" "Welcome!" "Hey don't you play at Cabaret Dante?" "Porter, do you know Zeke?"

Porter realizes that he is shaking. For a brief moment he

imagines that the whole lot of them are cannibals, playing out an elaborate hoax for his benefit, that the musician is to be the Thanksgiving meal. Or maybe Porter himself is.

"I'm gonna get some champagne," he barks. "We'll need it." He darts down the stairs, three spiraling stories, and out the heavy double doors to the street. Above him, the roommates fall to silence, nonplussed; amused but afraid to offend by admitting it. Zeke stares after Porter, silently injured.

Berlin laughs, waves a hand at the staircase. "Is supper started? Do you need help? We need to eat these beignets, they're disgusting cold. And I need some coffee."

They move inside.

They finish the beignets and coffee, spiking the coffee with brandy until it's depleted, then drinking just the brandy. The boys slam pans around in the kitchen, arguing over whether there is sugar in a pie crust while the girls show Zeke Berlin's book of photos and make him play Kirk's bass for them. The apartment fills with the warmth of cooked turkey and pumpkin pie, the energy of new friends and captivating, candid conversation.

As the turkey cools on the counter indoors, Porter stands outside in the chilly gray day. He gazes up at his balcony, wondering if he can climb to it. Sneak in. Unfortunately, his is not a gallery, does not have poles extending to the sidewalk and therefore offers no easy way to scale it. He concedes that he will have to climb the stairs like a normal person. He does not have even the buffer of a few bottles of champagne, because he had not yet put his wallet in his pants before he fled.

He cringes as he flings open the apartment doors.

"Here he is!" "Thank God! We can finally eat!" "I hope you didn't buy any more liquor because we've still got Kirk's vodka and Zeke brought a bottle of wine." "Yeah, we're saturated!"

"That's good," Porter admits. "The liquor store, I mean, I

forgot and —"

Alexis smiles in a way that makes him stop talking. Devlin puts some jazz on the sound system, while Candice and Kirk shuffle Porter to the head of the table. He observes, as they sit down together, their matched, coy ability, like a pair of healthy alley cats.

Berlin sits the musician on Porter's left, and she takes the seat to his right. They all raise glasses and she toasts: "To Thanksgiving with friends!"

"And no family!" Candice calls. Then to Berlin, "at least not mine."

Porter notices that Zeke puts his napkin in his lap, and eats with one hand beneath the table. Too mannered, too polished. Porter decides that the bassist, like so many folks down here in New Orleans, is running from the law.

"This is so good!" "Excellent." "Compliments to the chefs." "Why isn't it cheves?"

"Tell Zeke about your play." Berlin's eyes sparkle at Porter.

Porter hesitates. The roommates all seem to gaze at him, anticipating that he will remain silent. "It's about two people who keep trying to leave each other but they can't," he blurts. Bold, defiant.

Alexis breaks into song: "Try to say goodbye and I choke . . ."

"We should be so lucky!" Devlin laughs, wrapping an arm around her. His nose wrinkles.

" . . . try to walk away and I stumble . . . "

Porter frowns into his salad. "It's not like that."

"Is it absurdist?" Zeke asks. "Like Beckett, where they're always saying 'I'm going,' and never do, never intend to?"

Porter stares at the musician, mouth open. "A bit, yeah." He sets down his fork, curls a fist against his mouth and rests his elbow on the table. "Yeah, it's a bit like Beckett. You read?"

He catches Berlin's glare.

"Becket, I mean."

Zeke becomes quite interested in his turkey leg. "Much? Oh, no, no. Just the standards. Godot and Endgame."

"Any Chekhov?"

Zeke starts to nod but then glances up, hesitates. Berlin interrupts.

"He's hoping you haven't. My brother prides himself on hanging out with people less educated than he is. A simple enough task, given his scholarship."

"That was a bit of a backhand compliment." Alexis pours herself another glass of wine.

Porter pulls his elbow off the table. "I'll take a compliment anyway it's diced. Especially from her."

Berlin holds up her glass for a refill. "The danger, of course, is that he begins to believe his own hype. Perhaps if he paid some attention, he'd find that his play is on his own balcony. As it stands, he's surrounded by life-lusting luminaries, yet he chooses to write about hopeless hordes."

"Hopeless hordes." Porter purses his lips, nods. "That's good, did you rehearse that?"

"No, I didn't. Like the bumper sticker says, life is not a dress rehearsal."

Devlin shakes his fork. "Come on now, kids."

"See, this is why I say no family." To Berlin, Candice says, "No offence."

Zeke squirms in his seat, then springs from it, escapes to the kitchen. "Anybody else need water?"

"Can I see you in my room, please?" Porter mutters through his teeth.

"No."

"I mean it, Berlin."

"So do I. Here's your stage. Improvise."

Porter's eyes hood. In his head, images rise, flicker and get replaced like a sticking video stream: Berlin alight in her boa, giggling and dirty with the Cabaret girls, in private and dirtier with the musician.

"Where were you last night?"

"Where do you think?"

"You were out fucking him!" Porter singles out Zeke with a dead-level arm.

"I'd fuck him," Candice offers. "He's hot."

Kirk nods in affirmation. "She's right, Porter. You are hot, Zeke. I'd fuck you too."

"How about we smoke before sex?" Alexis stands, takes Zeke's arm and leads him to foyer, pulling him from the fray. Her roommates follow.

Berlin addresses her brother. "Zeke taught me how to play chess."

Porter scowls at his sister. "I've never heard it called that before."

"The knight moves in an L. The pawn can advance two spaces on his first move only."

He wants to shake her, slap her face, kiss her mouth. He wants to hurl her off the balcony and watch her bleed in the street; he wants to frame her and hang her on the wall.

In the foyer, Zeke is pacing. "Maybe I should go."

"Naw," says Candice, "they need to fight."

Kirk nods. "It's been building up all week."

"They grew up in separate houses, so they're making up for lost time."

"You ask me," Alexis says, hopping into the frame of the open window, "he wants her for himself." She lights a cigarette.

"That's disgusting!" Candice yelps. She's shushed by the lot of them.

The argument in the dining room has degraded the way arguments do.

"You're so manipulative and arrogant, and everybody thinks you're so great!"

"What if I am great?"

"Then you wouldn't parade around telling everybody what to do and screwing nameless musicians like some two-bit whore."

"Jealous?"

"The worst part is, I don't even think you like him. I think you did it just to spite me!"

"Are you aware, you have an extraordinarily high opinion of yourself?"

Alexis gestures. "She's right, he is jealous. I'm telling you—"

"That's disgusting."

"That's not how I mean it! Not sexually. He wants—"

"—her to recognize him." Kirk says this watching the siblings.

Suddenly, Berlin is in the living room, black duffle slung over her shoulder. "Why?" she snaps at her brother. "Because you'll look stupid if I go? You are stupid!"

"Piss off!"

She unzips a pocket on the big canvas bag and yanks from it a smallish, leather-bound book, a journal. "Here's your manuscript. Your play."

"What are you doing with that?"

She hurls it at him. "What do you care? You haven't looked at it in a week! I know because that's how long I've had it."

"It's none of your damn business what—"

"Shut up! For two minutes, just shut! Up!"

They glare at each other for a sudden, silent moment.

"It's a good play, Porter. Finish it. Then maybe you can stop acting like an asshole."

She crosses the threshold to the foyer, stops in front of Zeke. "I need a place to stay for a few days. Apparently, I'll fuck you for it."

Zeke's eyes flit from Berlin to her brother. His face is wide with apology and red with shame.

"Let her stay with you," Alexis assures him.

Devlin concurs. "We'll come over tomorrow and make you breakfast!"

Berlin and Zeke clomp down the staircase and Porter thinks he can make out every step, and which one of them is hitting it. He opens his journal. Berlin has added comments, made suggestions. In fierce red, she's crossed out "husband and wife," written in "brother and sister." Struck through "New Jersey," scribbled: "Where's your heart?"

Porter charges to his room, where he tosses open the doors. It's raining! Water falls chill and stinging, making the rails cold and slippery under his bare feet. Peering into the distance, he can see two forms jogging down his street towards Decatur. One wears only a white tank-top, carries a large black bag, the other has a flannel draped over her head.

The rain falls harder: Big drops pat, pat, pat in cold splotches against the street, ping off the balcony. Porter holds open his hand, arm outstretched like a beggar.

Come Saturday, he knows, Zeke will be on his knees: Stay with me. His roommates will be whining "Stay with us!" All New Orleans will have its hand out, just as Porter does now to the glorious rain. But Berlin is just passing through.

His sister, she's the one who leaves.

Ares in His Mad Fits Knows No Favorites

My friend Hampton stands in the shallow end of her apartment pool, munching Mo' Better Cheesy Cheese Puffs and reading the bag. The green Cheese Puff bag matches her green bikini and the lifeguard keeps watching her. I know he likes her, because she's not supposed to be eating inside the actual pool like that, but he's staring right at her, not saying a word. I'd guess his mind is on other things.

I'm stretched out on a towel, drying off from my recent foray into the water, and struggling my way through The Odyssey. It's about two hundred degrees outside today, plus it's humid, so it feels about three hundred. Hampton's mom bitches at us if we stay in and run the air conditioner all day, so we poured some of her hard lemonade into big blue plastic cups, got some snacks, and headed to the pool.

Hampton pretty much always gets the cheese puffs, but I like spicy foods, so I usually get Mo' Better Hott-Hott-Hott fries, but I don't eat 'em inside the pool because I'm not built like Hampton. I don't even own a bikini.

I highlight some text and annoy myself by getting water

on the book when Hampton interrupts me. "Hey, Tarah, listen to this!"

I sigh loudly. "I'm trying to finish this stupid poem—"

"It's an epic, not just a poem."

"—for this stupid AP class. That you made us take!"

"Oh, please! My tiny violin is inside."

"My last summer in high school, and this is how I'm spending it."

She laughs at me. "Sulking, you mean?"

"Take Summer Session World Literature with me, she says—"

Hampton throws a handful of cheese puffs at me.

"It'll be fun, she says. She lies!"

"You're only struggling with it because you refuse to even try and like it."

"I did so try! It's boring."

"It's gorier than a horror movie! How is that boring to you?"

"The women are treated like cattle."

"Chattel. And anyhow, I'd think the fact of your being Greek would lend the story some inherent . . . that you'd be inherently interested in it."

The truth is, Hampton can't fathom that somebody could not be interested in any book, but especially a classic. That's how I met her, way back in fifth grade. I was getting off the bus and she smacked me in the back of the head—with a book!

"Ow!" I cried this out of annoyance, not pain, and I could tell by her pursed lips that she knew it.

"I wanna read that." She pointed to my slender black paperback, A Hero Ain't Nothing but a Sandwich. "I'll trade you for mine." She held hers up for my scrutiny. A Tree Grows in Brooklyn.

Thick as a brick, her novel. Clearly a challenge. I couldn't not accept.

That book, I liked. Loved, even! But this Odyssey business?

"Maybe it is interesting, I can't tell because I can't get past the ridiculous, unpronounceable names!"

"How ironic. Tarah Persephone Kokinos. Your middle name is in the book! She's a goddess."

"It's not a book, it's an epic. Poem.

She dismisses me with a wave of her orange-grit covered fingers. "Right now, it's all inconsequential. Listen to this." She holds up the Mo' Better Cheesy Cheese Puff Bag and reads from the back of it: "Contains natural and artificial flavors and colors and Yellow Number Five." She peers over the bag. "Natural and artificial colors aaa-yannd . . . Yellow Number Five. What does that mean exactly? If it's not either of those, what is it?"

"Supernatural?" I offer. "Paranormal?"

"Something."

She upends the bag and empties it into her mouth. Around a mouthful of crumbs she tells me, "I say it needs investigating."

Which is why, despite my plans to be an engineer while Hampton wants to go to college for English, we still boast a seven-year friendship that's weathered a combined five boyfriends, one failed algebra class, one broken arm, and the deaths of two dogs, a cat, and one grandparent.

"Adventure Girls?" I ask to be sure.

"Adventure Girls!"

"Now that, I can agree to!" I close my World Literature book, calling out our slogan: "Wear comfortable shoes!"

"Bring a towel!" Hampton answers.

Together: "And always pack snacks!"

Around laughter I ask Hampton, "How should we start?"

She examines the back of the bag again. "Ah! Website."

She thrusts the bag at me. "Look it up."

She means on my phone but, "My phone's dead, remember?"

"Oh, right." She frowns and looks away. Her dad stopped paying for her phone a few months ago, when her folks split up and he moved out. That's another thing we've weathered. But she doesn't say too much about it. No more phone, no more ski club, plus now she lives in an apartment. She lived in a house before. I guess that says enough.

"We could use my mom's computer," I offer.

Hampton turns back to me with a big smile. "Okay!" She swishes her hands around in the pool. The lifeguard whistle blows, but he is pointing at some kids messing around in the deep end.

We dry off perfunctorily, toss shorts over our suits and then ride our bikes over to my place. Like Hampton, I live with just my mom, but we got the house. Hampton's dad had their home computer—her mom only has a work laptop. I guess the home computer stayed with the home.

I start Mom's PC, log us in, then turn over the keyboard to Hampton. She punches in the web address from the back of her green bag. Mo' Better! proclaim neat, cursive letters. What Mo' could you want? Their gold-on-green logo is like a college sports team, each letter bigger than the last.

Hampton finds her cheese puffs under "products." But the page for them says nothing about the ingredients. "This is just a big ad," she complains.

"Duh. What do you think the Web is for? Do a search on Yellow Number Five."

This returns a bunch of sites for a band with that name, and a few FDA hits. She checks out the FDA site, but it only tells us about safety and toxicity, not how the stuff is made. There are some sites that supply the dye, but they don't reveal the ingredients either.

"Hey look at this!"

I do. It's some hoopla over the stuff apparently causing impotency.

"Who cares? We're not boys."

Hampton shrugs in agreement. "Probably urban legend anyway."

She clicks the back button about sixty times to get back to the Mo' Better site. "They must have a phone number." Finally she gets there and I'm proud of myself for not snatching the mouse out of her hand.

"Hey! These snacks are manufactured right here."

"Huh?"

She taps the bottom of the screen with a shiny blue fingernail. There are very tiny letters there, as if the website is whispering a secret. "The Mo' Better factory. It's right downtown!"

I shove her. "The address is on the bag!"

She shoves me back. "No it isn't! Just the distributor! And they're in Chicago."

I peer at the address on the screen, thinking it was probably on the bag, or this address must be the web designer but no, it says for Mo' Correspondence, and it's not a post office box, either. There is a phone number, as well.

"Call 'em!"

I hand her the cordless and she dials. Up until her dad left, she made a point to tell me how hilarious it was that we still have a landline. Now, they have one, too.

After a long moment of listening, she frowns, pulls the phone from her ear and punches a number. She listens, then frowns harder. "They don't have any kind of technical support option."

"What do they have?"

"If I need to speak to a certain person or if I'm interested in being a Mo' Better distributor."

"Pick the second one."

She punches another button. While she's listening, I examine my Hott-Hott-Hott Fries and discover that they too contain this yellow mystery substance.

Hampton hangs up, utterly scowling.

"Whatsa' matter?"

"It's a wonder these people manage to sell their products at all, given the amount of duress one is put through trying to become a distributor."

"Like I said, whatsa' matter?"

"They want me to leave a message."

"So? Leave one."

"Are you performing slightly below your normal mental capacity today, Tarah?"

"What! Leave a message, they call you back."

Her mouth forms a line and she crosses her arms. "They return the call, thinking we're a retail store. What if your mom answers?"

"She's not even home till after five. You've had too much to drink or something. Leave a damn message."

She peers into the monitor again. "Nope. This requires more aggressive tactics. We're going there."

"Wouldn't it make more sense to ask the guys who make the stuff? The dye, I mean."

"Perhaps. But the dye manufacturer doubtlessly gets harassed about its alien pigment regularly, and therefore has a spin-doctored pre . . . ah, they'll be defensive and lie. Besides, we can't just drive down to the Mo' Yellow Yellow Number Five factory. "

"We don't have a car, Hampton. We can't just drive to the Cheesy Cheese Puff factory either! We may as well be trying to get to the FDA itself. You know, in Washington?"

"Don't be absurd. The bus surely runs into the industrial sector. Check!"

Sure enough, it does. In fact, "It's only two buses. One right up the street, on the Boulevard, then an exchange at the main terminal."

Still, I'm thinking this is ridiculous. Maybe even dangerous; I've never been into the city, not to that part of it, where the factories are. But Hampton is raring.

"It doesn't make any sense!" She shakes the Cheese Puff bag at me. "No sense at all!" I'm pretty sure she's talking about more than Yellow Number Five. Even though she might not know it.

Ever since Hampton's dog died, she won't kill spiders, or even house centipedes. Everything gets scooped up and taken outside now. And ever since her dad left, she needs the why of everything.

It's like all of life has become a big Sudoku puzzle, and if she can determine the correct answer to some of the "easy" boxes, eventually even those ones that could have five different possible answers will reveal themselves. One of those boxes is her dad taking off. I guess she's thinking—or hoping—Yellow Number Five is an easy box.

So I figure why not go, I can even study on the bus. (Though I'd rather do Sudoku!) If you've ever studied on a shock-less, moving vehicle, you know that I am a fool for trying. It is with a vandalized copy of The Odyssey and a raging headache that I tumble off the bus.

Into hell itself. The industrial area of our city is dirty and neglected. Squat brick buildings sit on expansive plots of scraggly land. Farther up, the buildings get darker and taller, the grass completely displaced by concrete and asphalt. At night these streets must be desolate except for people looking to make real trouble. We step off the bus into the hot sun and I'm glad it's only two o'clock and summer; we'll be back before dark.

"This way," Hampton tells me, and we start walking.

The streets reek of heat and asphalt. When we reach the third block, we learn why: freshly laid black goo emanating its pungent scent. Looking across it, the buildings in the distance ripple and sway. The smell makes everything seem hotter.

"Are you sure you got the address right?" I bark at Hampton.

"Yes. But we've got another three blocks to go." She points to the top of a slight incline, three city blocks up. "There it is."

The collegiate hunter-green and gold Mo' Better banner sits at the top of the slope. I concede and trudge up the hill behind her.

"I want a soda," I whine.

"I'm sure they have a snack machine inside."

That thought makes me happy enough, and I'm silent for the rest of the hike. The Mo' Better sign shimmers in the distance like the buildings did, and all I can think about is the lovely, lovely soda machine which I will put money into—crumpled dollar bills of salvation—and in return get a nice cold wet drink and then maybe get another. Will I get cola? Or orange? Really, it's best to start with clear soda if you're—

"Shhh!" Hampton stops in front of me and I nearly run into her.

"I wasn't saying anything!"

She purses her lips at me. "Listen!"

First, all I hear is how quiet it is, the way you'd expect a Sunday to be. But it's Wednesday, so it's creepy. Then I hear a commotion. Voices—some angry, some pleading.

Hampton cocks her head. "I think it's from there." She points to the Mo' Better building. "Come on!"

Now she's running. Of course she is, she's wearing a bikini top, not a clammy, clingy oversized T-shirt, plus she's not carrying a ten-pound textbook for an extra-credit class her moron friend convinced her to take and that she hates. Dammit.

I trot after her. But I'm sweating and it's muggy and I stop, just walk. Trot, walk, trot the rest of the way, until I get to where Hampton crouches—the corner of the dead, gray building next to our target. Mere yards from us stands the Mo' Better factory, a windowless brick box. The taller structures of granite and steel surrounding it make it seem anachronistic.

Hampton sees I've caught up to her and scurries away again, jogging through the corridor formed by the two factories. Mo' Better's neighbor looms like a ghost ship, a gray tower with blackened, busted out windows and a for-sale sign crouching on its brown lawn.

A fence meets the back of the building, running parallel to separate the two lots. I scrutinize the "fence," an askew collection of rotted wooden planks held vaguely vertical by some drooping chicken wire. A tangle of barbed wire crowns it all.

The thick air conveys the sound of what is now clearly an argument, I can hear it between my panted breaths.

"Let's go back!" I hiss.

But Hampton either doesn't hear or ignores me. She squirrels between the building and the chicken wire. I peer through this tiny gap and watch her scrabble along the fence. At least the rotted planks conceal her from the view of whoever is fighting in the Mo' Better yard.

I take a deep breath. Squeezing through, I follow her, but I keep glancing up. I'm convinced the barbed wire is going to finally give way after all these years, and tumble and shred me.

Vintage TV Cop-Show music plays in my head. I don't know what we expect to find—two guys with knives, tied to each other? A ring of people huddled around chickens? Maybe a thick cloud of Yellow Number Five fumes, scandalously poisoning the entire region.

The alley between the two industrial buildings opens to a yard filled mostly by train tracks. They look maintained, might still be in use. Beyond them is a filthy, barren field, choked with tall weeds and the victim of illegal dumping: Couches, kitchen cabinets, a car carcass.

The fence stops here, just three feet from the tracks, and we crouch down, peer through spaces between the disintegrating planks. The Mo' Better factory is only half the length of the decayed structure whose yard we're in, and the fence has led us out another block. Sure enough, from here we can see the source of the yelling.

Moving diagonally across the Mo' Better lot, toward the field and toward us, is a group of five people, six if you include the dead guy. How do I know he's dead? Well, it's a guess. But there's two guys carrying his bloody body, and another guy carrying his arm.

The four of them—the pallbearers and the dead guy—all wear uniforms, dark green pants and striped, short-sleeved shirts with the Mo' Better logo swathed across the back.

A fifth man lags behind; his open striped shirt revealing his taut chest. He yelps and hollers, his English heavily accented— he sounds like my last Math teacher Mr. Sarraf, who was from Yemen.

His grievances carry through the static heat. ". . . How you can just dump him, ah? Like some animal? Some dog or what? Ah! He is your brother-in-law!" Anger reddens his bronze face.

"He's illegal!"

The man answering wears a suit, dark green, and a gold tie. His accent is milder, some kind of Spanish, Puerto Rican maybe. He's got a voice like he swallowed a Buick—growly and ferocious.

"He's illegal and he's dead," the suited man snarls. "Now, I no longer know him. Now I can't know him." He follows behind the three men carrying the body, his angry employee nipping at his heels.

"And what your sister, you tell?" the small man challenges. Rage distorts his face and burns in his shiny black eyes.

The suit stops, the burial party keeps moving. "They begged me for a job, I gave him a job. I owed them nothing. I could have said no."

"Maybe'd be better. He'd be alive, maybe. How are we safe now? Us working for you."

The suit considers the smaller man. The big one has sweated through his jacket, and his nostrils flare with each labored breath.

"Accidents happen. God knows why. We do not. My sister will be taken care of. You don't want to work for me anymore? Then quit. But your mouth better stay shut." A thick finger sticks the smaller man in the chest, pushes him backward. "Or you'll be taken care of as well, mi amigo."

The little man glares, shaking. Finally he spits on the suited man's shoes. "Ya ibn asharmoota!"

A truck rumbles by. Panic breaks over my morbid fascination, I feel clammy, and my heart beats in my throat. I see that Hampton is trembling, and I grab her arm.

Before she finishes nodding, she's following me back along the fence, past the dead building, onto the street.

She grabs my hand and we slap! slap! slap! down the hill, past the smelly asphalt and its shimmering heat. We gallop three city blocks from the slaughtered man, his living conscience, and his stony brother-in-law.

Finally, finally into the bus shelter. I sit. Hampton paces.

We shiver in the heat, waiting for the bus.

Hampton curses and gripes a lot. "Where is it? I swear it's been an hour!"

I flip the pages of my fat textbook, chew my nails and mutter. "Did they see us? Are they coming? Jesus."

Our eyes continually glance up the hill. From here, inside the shelter, not even the Mo' Better flag is visible.

No one comes. The streets stay empty, save delivery trucks and the mailman. When the bus appears in the distance, I'm afraid to believe it. "What if it's not ours?"

"Shut up."

But it is, it's ours, and I'm so relieved that I don't even mind how the murky cold inside nauseates me after the triple digit heat, or how I have to pee so bad it hurts, I don't even care.

There's almost nobody on the bus. We take the bench seats in the back, sitting across from each other. I stare out the window while the bus belches and rumbles its way past the squat buildings and scraggly lots. Two or three people get on at each stop. Nobody gets off. Finally the houses appear. Soon we'll be at the station, where we'll transfer, and take our bus back to the safety of the suburbs. The entire trip will cover maybe twenty miles, taking just over an hour.

I am speculating how far the dead man traveled to be struck down by his brother-in-law's machinery, how far it might be from his home to here. The book I'm clutching and my assigned story seem insignificant now, so simple that I am ashamed to have been complaining.

I envision men in the field. As I do, a fragment comes to me, a description from the textbook's introduction. ". . . he personified the physical valor obligatory for success in war, and was a frenzied force; irrational, insatiable, destructive and slaughtering."

Ares.

I glance at Hampton. Her gaze finds me, and we both smile, nervous, relieved. Then laugh. We laugh, and laugh, and laugh.

We don't say it but we know: We are lucky. We are privileged.

"No more Mo' Better," Hampton says. Her only words for the duration of the ride.

I set my bedraggled textbook in my lap, hoping in the future we have more than a petty boycott as our thunderbolt against Chaos. Fearing, as grownups like to tell us, that these are in fact our finest days. But certain, at least, that while the gods— or whatever larger force—may indeed know our fortunes and our fate, we don't. And can't, and never will.

The High Price of the Wild Truth

Jackson Blake's grandfather rattled off his usual morning litany, emphasizing his imminent death and the likelihood of it resulting from the rotten food at the nursing home. "Then they'll close all the doors, how they do. How's a closed door gonna save us from death? They don't even lock 'em! As if—" He stopped abruptly. The old man leaned forward, squinted his wrinkly eyes and peered at his grandson. With a concern Jackson hadn't heard since his grammar-school days nearly thirty years ago, the old man asked, "What happened to your face, kid?"

It was the third in a series of events convincing Jackson that the world was destined for swift and soon destruction. His Grandfather's Sudden Reversion, the Perfumed Woman in the elevator, and the Coyote. These formed, in Jackson's mind, an ominous triumvirate.

He raised a hand to his swollen lip and bruised cheek and eye. At least his nose wasn't broken. Jackson liked his nose. "A Greco-Roman nose," TV Guide's Adam Fitzpatrick had once said about it, "classic and expressive." Jackson was glad not to have had his expressive nose busted.

His four-year "Face of a Handsome Boxer" epithet had taken on a new meaning last night. He'd assumed his grandfather wouldn't see it, just like he couldn't see the television or the crosswords anymore. "I was helping my neighbor move."

"That's not a helping-your-neighbor-move face. That's a got-busted-with-your-neighbor's-wife face."

"Not exactly."

What to tell Grampa Pedro?

At three in the morning, Jackson had been awakened by an odd and un-placeable noise—like glass breaking in slow motion. He peered through his peephole and saw his immediate upstairs neighbor poised on the upper landing. The cement stairs led down to Jackson's doorstep, and Mel—the neighbor—clutched a giant pink crayon and gaped sadly at Jackson's door. Which Jackson opened.

"What's wrong Mel?" The giant crayon functioned as a coin bank, as evidenced by the ankle-deep pile of assorted change that cascaded onto his feet. "Mel" was Melvina, Jackson's dress-wearing, male-appearing neighbor who preferred to be called "she."

"Sshhhh!" In a harsh whisper, Melvina told Jackson: "I'm sneaking out. I can't pay the rent and I don't want to be evicted."

"So you're moving out at two in the morning? You—"

"SHHH!"

Jackson whispered back, "You don't even have a car!"

"I called a cab; it's waiting outside. I'm taking what fits in it. I was going to take my crayon, you know, but . . ." Melvina gestured helplessly at the shiny mess at the bottom of the stairs.

"If you cashed that all in you could probably pay your rent!"

"I need it for groceries. Besides, I found a cheaper place. In Hollywood."

Jackson questioned the existence of a cheaper place than their fifty-five-unit North Hollywood barrio building.

"East of Vine," Melvina explained.

After making Melvina promise not to become a prostitute, Jackson helped his neighbor refill the pink crayon as quietly as possible, by first pushing all the coins into his studio apartment and then scooping them back into the bank.

"I thought you had a job." Jackson dropped a handful of coins into the mouth of the giant cardboard crayon. Its point came off, which made filling it easier. The bottom also came off, which Melvina hadn't known until a few minutes ago.

"I got fired," she sulked. "They caught me working on my novel at my desk. But I got my work done. It's not like anybody who came into the office would ever know I wasn't working on an article or something. I think it's sexism."

Jackson glanced at Melvina's five o'clock shadow, and "her" hairy, unshaved legs, visible past her knee-length floral tank-dress. Melvina wasn't what Jackson thought of a transsexual. To Jackson, Melvina barely qualified as a transvestite. To Jackson, Melvina was simply a man in a dress.

"Sexism?"

"People think it's over, but far from it. Believe you me!" She winked.

Jackson let it go. Melvina was odd, but intelligent and funny, and the only friend Jackson had made in the six months since he'd moved from bourgeois-artsy Central Coast. So he helped Melvina get the last of her few things—a suitcase and a lamp—while the cab meter ticked. Then Jackson gave her the business card of the Perfumed Woman from the elevator, advising Melvina to be honest about why she'd been fired. "You can tell her I sent you if you want. And tell her you're good with phones. And you don't like research."

"Thank you sooo much," Melvina gushed gruffly. "I wish I could buy you lunch or something. I'll email you a copy of the novel! No one else has seen it yet, not even my agent."

Jackson agreed that'd be great.

So he had been helping his neighbor move. But that's not what earned him the shiner.

He'd tried going back to sleep, but the bar in his fold-out couch had seemed especially uncomfortable. Or maybe it was the heat. Three—no, four—in the morning and the temperature still hung in triple digits. He missed the ocean, wished he had some vodka. Or weed. Or heroin or gasoline. Instead he found his book—Haruki Murakami's Wild Sheep Chase. Jackson had loved private investigator books since childhood, when he'd read himself to sleep under the sheets with a flashlight. Tonight, though, just as the sandman came calling, another commotion dragged him from bed. This was a more familiar noise.

Tanya lived upstairs, next door to Melvina. She and Melvina swapped quick-and-easy-recipes, and Tanya tried to provide Melvina tips on how to be more feminine. But while Melvina sequestered herself away (apparently to write a book), Tanya had a string of bad boyfriends. There'd been musicians, actors, a crooked judge who turned up dead, a handsome Persian prince who got deported, and a doctor who seemed promising until he was arrested for writing phony pain-med prescriptions.

Now some new clown hollered in the hallway while she shushed him. Jackson squinted into his peep hole again. This time he saw Tanya on the landing, pinned against the wall by some lumbering suit. Suit's hand kept pushing her skirt up her thigh and hers kept pushing his back down. Finally she squirmed away from him. "I think it's better if you go."

Her date laughed. "We been together three weeks, and it's time I get me a little somethin' somethin'."

SLAP! "I'll give you a little something!"

Their scuffle took them out of Jackson's limited view. Should he do something? It meant admitting he'd been spying. A snippet of his TV show's opening song surfaced to memory: *"Always help the helpless . . ."*

Other guys had their college-days radio music, Jackson had his theme song. He sang through it silently *"Always help the helpless, never fear the fearless, be doubtful of the doubtless, give the penniless your change . . ."* he hummed his way through the bridge, then heard a small whine and a dull thud followed by chilling quiet.

He tossed open his door. "Tanya?"

He could see her legs sprawled awkwardly on the landing, the rest of her obscured by her kneeling date.

The Suit turned and snarled at him. "Mind your own damn business!"

Jackson jolted up the stairs. Some temporary insanity, the heat or exhaustion, made him grab Tanya's six-feet-plus date by his immense shoulders. He yanked backwards, sent Suit tumbling. Suit tumbled all the way back onto to his feet and out the door, grumbling curses and threats.

Tanya pulled herself to consciousness. She saw a man standing over her and slugged him in the face with everything she had. That man, of course, was Jackson. And what Tanya had was a full bottle of scotch. A kinder world would have given Jackson a new friend. One that shared her liquor. Instead, Tanya's confusion or embarrassment sent her lunging up the stairs, where she slammed her door in Jackson's face.

So what to tell his grandfather? Did it even matter? The old man believed and remembered what he wanted. That's why Jackson was the only one taking care of him now.

"I was helping a neighbor move and her boyfriend showed up," Jackson said. "They had a fight and he seemed pretty out of control."

Grampa Pedro scrutinized him again. Jackson expected the usual rattle-your-chain treatment, something like *Helping her move—is that what the kids call it these days? Ha ha! You got what you had coming, boy!* But instead, Grampa rested his chin in his hand.

"Playing the hero is stupid, kid. But real nice. That's nice what you did. I guess that's what you were known for. In your day, I mean."

Jackson wondered if his grandfather felt all right. But before he could ask, one of the nurses appeared in the doorway. "There's our Mister Sailor," she jingled. Grampa Pedro cringed at her voice. "Breakfast is ready," she told Jackson.

Jackson wheeled his grandfather to the dining room, then slipped away quickly, before the horror of old age had a chance to crash over him. Once-dignified people who could no longer hold a fork, who were made to wear bibs just like babies—it struck Jackson as a cruel, nasty end to a too-short life.

The elevator reeked of whatever horrible preprocessed food they'd brought up for the residents. Not like yesterday, Saturday morning, when it had smelled sweetly musky, like sex and leather and expensive cigars, reminding him of his agent's office. Yesterday, he'd waited an extra-long time, which Jackson had found confusing since the arrow told him the elevator was headed down and his grandfather lived on the top floor. When it opened, a woman appeared. Quite a woman.

Her height struck him first, above his own five-eleven. Then her hair, wine red and down past her hips, even in a complex braid. Godiva, he thought. *I've met Lady Godiva in the elevator.* Jackson stepped inside, needlessly pressed the button for the lobby and then stared at the floor.

"You look familiar." Her voice matched her opulent scent.

"Maybe you've seen me around the home," he suggested.

"That's not it." Her confidence impressed him. "Turn sideways?"

He laughed but did as requested.

She squinted at him. "Say: 'Consider your ticket punched.'"

He repeated the phrase dully.

"Say it right!" she implored, and they both laughed.

"You busted me." He grinned at her.

She smiled back, her violet eyes gleaming. "That was a good show. Why'd they cancel it?"

The show she referred to was Ferryman. He'd played the starring role, Jared Ferryman, a hitman's hitman. His first killing had been to avenge his father, after proclaiming he'd never follow in his father's gun-for-hire footsteps. Of course, one thing led to another, and every episode had him killing somebody. It was a dark comedy; Jared was a Melrose grunge kid with a tribal neck tattoo and an attitude bigger than a house.

The show predated Six Feet Under and Nip/Tuck and even the Sopranos, and had been a hit with critics and audiences alike. Still, "Egos got in the way. MGM picked it up for a movie, which they filmed but never released because Tommie—Tomas Jacobs over at Fox?—he just hated me." Jackson shrugged. "You know how it goes."

"What are you doing now?"

"I seem to have a penchant for getting fired."

The elevator stopped. The woman exited but didn't continue to the entranceway. "Who fires the famous?"

"Debt collectors, the Los Angeles Times subscription department, movie survey people. This month."

"Not good with phones?"

"Not good with people. After my show was canceled, I took the money and ran to Central Coast. Found an investor who keeps me in buttons and bows, and I stay up with the trees and the fish, where it's safe. But then Grandpa got sick, and the money's not enough to cover a place here and . . ." Jackson trailed off, at once saddened by his pathetic state and startled by his own sudden garrulousness. Something in this woman, her impossible colors and her chocolate voice, worked on him like strong liquor.

"How are you with stuff—objects? Good?"

"I'd say so, yeah."

A business card materialized. "If you'd like a job—testing things—phone me. I can use more people in R and D."

Jackson took the card, which was made to look as though forged from steel, complete with rivets. A sharp, raised S sat in the center, the ubiquitous S Jackson saw everywhere. But he'd assumed the company an urban myth which in actuality only made clothing.

"Survivanoia. You make actual stuff?"

"Like you wouldn't believe." Her eyes sparkled.

"I've got a baseball cap by you guys. Lead lined, you know."

"Do you like it?"

"Sure. I haven't, like, needed it."

"You mean you haven't been shot at yet."

Jackson nodded. The fact of such a sophisticated woman so unflinchingly able to discuss violence set him off kilter.

"Well, now you can get paid to find out if it works." She strolled out the sliding doors, leaving Jackson with alarming images of himself bent over double in his lead-lined, supposedly bullet-resistant baseball cap while somebody took aim at his head.

Then the woman shot him a toothy grin over her shoulder that startled and shocked him. Because, what, with those perfect teeth and the red hair and that clever, daring grin, she looked just like the Coyote. The Coyote had started it all, Saturday morning.

Saturday mornings are sleepier than weekdays. Jackson went to visit his grandfather every morning, though, and always before breakfast. Sometimes, if he was feeling especially generous, he'd go in the evening as well, but he always went before breakfast no matter how grumpy. Jackson and the dayworkers were the only people awake most Saturdays.

Yesterday had started out typical. He first picked up coffee and a newspaper for Grampa Pedro, a trip that, as usual, brought him to the broad intersection on Ventura Boulevard right where the bookstore and Ishmael's are located.

All the lights hung red for a moment. And then, the coyote caught Jackson's eye. It strolled through the lawns of wealthy southside residents and paused, peering up at the traffic signal. The signal changed in the coyote's favor, and the animal jaunted across Ventura and off to do business. Eat cats and carry off babies, Jackson had figured.

Jackson's now-deceased brother, Carl, had adored coyotes, said they were "really excellent." He'd once expounded on their extensive appearance in Native American mythology. At the stoplight, Jackson recalled none of it, only the pain of his loss. But seeing the mythical little beast reflected in a beautiful, enigmatic woman's face brought something back. Jokesters and creators. Creatures who would play you for a fool to teach you a lesson.

Of course, he'd given her card to Melvina. Maybe Melvina would get taught the lesson. Like don't wear Old Spice if you plan to put on a dress! Here in the elevator, Jackson laughed to himself, but then felt glum. Melvina had been his only friend, and now she was gone.

The stench of the bad food nauseated him, muddled his already confused head.

He'd seen the Coyote and met the Perfumed Woman just yesterday. Looking back it felt like weeks. Earlier in the week he'd woken from vivid dreams he hadn't shaken until well after lunch, and his sleep patterns seemed to want to reverse, keep him in bed during the day and prowling the streets at night.

He'd mentioned the dreaming to Melvina, who first dismissed it as heat-related, then reconsidered and suggested Jackson's mind was turning in on itself as a result of isolation. Jackson pointed out that he'd been previously sequestered in Central Coast.

"It's not the same. You were isolated before because there was nothing around but the ocean and pine trees. Now you're surrounded by people. This isolation is the result of anonymity of a big city."

But Jackson wasn't quite anonymous either. Occasionally people recognized him from his show. Like the Perfumed Woman. No, Jackson fingered the heat as his problem, believed his planned drive to Zuma Beach would help.

He drove his red Miata up the steep curves of Topanga Canyon, top down, wind whipping his dark, wavy hair. He liked it wind-blown, disguising his graying temples. A few Harleys passed him on their way to the Rock Shop. A group of kids on Hondas buzzed by him too, leaning so low on the curves that Jackson chewed his lip, afraid for them. Aside from helmets, the kids wore no protective gear, no chaps, not even boots. There were dressed for the most part like Jackson, in knee-length rip-stop shorts, and ringer tank tops and sandals. He envied their moxie.

Once he got to the top of the canyon, a cool breeze hit him, and as he sped down the other winding side, the temperature dropped nearly twenty degrees. The chill cleared his head, and the sight of the ocean, even from so far up, soothed him instantly. Pacific Coast Highway was jammed with cars, full of everything from movie producers and their trophy wives to minivans of fat little kids. Zuma Beach was packed too, with no open spaces on the beach road. He had to park on the Highway, wait for a lull in traffic, then dart across four lanes.

The day's modest waves attracted twice the usual surfers, since newbies could catch them and not injure themselves, while veterans showed off and picked up chicks. Or guys—Jackson noted a significant number of the surfers were girls. Different from when he'd surfed. He'd never been any good but his TV self (naturally) surfed whenever he wasn't killing people or hanging out on Melrose being a smart-ass. Ah, the joy of television clichés.

Jackson stretched out on his towel and set to reading.

"Nice tattoo." A red-bikini clad girl with shoulder-length, salt- and sun-chewed hair blocked his light. "Does it mean something?"

She inspected the tribal band on his right biceps. Jackson had stolen the pattern from Jared Ferryman's neck tattoo. Superficially it appeared as any other tribal band, but closer inspection revealed the name Charon, and for the studious, the Greek version appeared as well.

"A friend of mine designed it," Jackson said. He watched her eyes steal a glance beyond the tattoo along the length of his taut frame.

She gave him a cute smile. "Anybody sitting here?"

"No, go ahead."

Jackson watched the girl, "I'm Stacey," unroll her Spiderman towel, and dig through a big red bag for some sunscreen. He figured her a kid, maybe twenty. Too young. Too bad. She smiled at him again, then caught sight of his left side, despite the visor and sunglasses. "Somebody beat you up. Oohhh." She pouted adorably. Jackson had forgotten the ability of a bruised face to garner attention and sympathy.

"You should see the other guy," he joked. Then added, "It looks worse than it feels," when she still appeared worried.

She frowned, unconvinced, but dropped the subject.

"Whatcha' reading?"

Jackson showed her his book.

"Translated! Are you a college student?"

"Naw. This is really just an old-fashioned P.I. novel. Well, sort of Raymond Chandler meets Don Delillo, you know? Gritty but introspective. "

She cocked her head at him, like he'd triggered some memory. "You look familiar."

He just shrugged, hoping her age meant she hadn't seen his show, that she mistook him for somebody else. This was why he avoided Santa Monica; all the German tourists were just now importing early 90s American television and they all recognized him.

So did she. "You're Jared Ferryman! Ohmigawd I loved your show when I was a kid! Wow, and you're a regular guy. At the beach." She dug a pen and a notebook out of her giant bag. "So you like that writer? Wild . . . Sheep . . . .a,m,i. What else do you read? Who'd you say, Raymond Armadillo?"

Jackson, grinning, corrected her. She charmed him. Was she by herself? Not exactly. "I'm here with my brother, but he just divorced his wife and doesn't want me around interfering with his macking." They talked about books—she liked Candice Bushnell and Steve Martin—sunscreened each other, and bodysurfed together for a while. Jackson felt light and happy, and began to wonder if Melvina had been right, that he needed somebody to play with.

As they trundled back to shore, an enormous wave crashed over them. The rush of cool water shoved Stacey off balance. Jackson grabbed her around the waist to keep her from going under. And then her mouth was pressed against his, soft and salty and warm. Nice. *She's too young* splashed through his mind. *This is wrong*. But it didn't feel wrong, it felt good. Another wave crashed over them and he pulled her against him.

Her mouth opened and her tongue brushed against his lips. Jackson yielded. He tugged her closer, nibbled her tongue and her mouth, felt a soft whimper escape her. Their kiss broke and she fell against him, sighed deeply, "Jared."

Oh.

In the moment, Jackson recognized the scene for the schoolgirl fantasy it was; Stacey's brother recognized his kid sister making out with some guy.

"Hey!" A gruff voice hollered over the surf's roar. Then splash splash splash and a stocky kid with hair identical to Stacey's had her by the wrists. But he chose to yell at Jackson, leave my sister alone! and all that. And she hollered back about leaving her by herself while he scoped hotties on the beach, and what's good for the goose.

Though reluctant to involve himself in some obvious long-running family dispute, Jackson felt obligated to defend his would-be girlfriend. He said something about her being an adult and making her own decisions.

"An adult? She's sixteen!"

Oh . . . hell.

Jackson rubbed his gray temples and cursed god while Stacey and her burly brother packed up her things and argued their way off the beach.

* * *

"Where've you been?" his Grandpa Pedro grumbled a morning greeting. "I thought you weren't coming this morning." As usual, he had wheeled himself to the lobby and vultured by the elevator door until Jackson arrived at his customary five a.m. Seemed he was back to grumpy, grouchy normal.

"I'm here same time as always. Here's your paper."

"Coffee?"

"Yeah, that too. You want to go to the big room?"

Grandpa Pedro's wizened head bobbed in agreement. Jackson handed him the two coffees to hold, grasped the back of the wheelchair and pushed slowly down the quiet length of the hallway.

The nursing home resembled a Vegas hotel with its garish carpet, gaudy wallpaper and wall sconces shaped like different flowers. It didn't quite smell like a hospital.

Jackson wheeled his grandfather into "the big room," a sort of conference room for old people, with two large glass dining room tables set up against each other and ringed by attractive but uncomfortable white wicker chairs. The room sat in the corner of the three-story building, looking out over the parking lot and the meticulous landscaping. Jackson arranged Grandpa Pedro so he could look out the window, even though the old man couldn't see past the length of his arm.

"So. How's your job going?" The same question Pedro asked every morning once they settled into the big room.

"Good," Jackson lied. "The same." For weeks he'd been lying, because he figured it was easier than explaining about getting fired repeatedly.

"You take a lot of orders, then?"

"Yup. Get a commission on every one."

"That's good. Not many places give a commission anymore." Grandpa Pedro thrust the paper at him. "Read me the obits, would ya? Make sure I'm still alive to drink this coffee."

Jackson dutifully read the obituary section aloud, just the names. On occasion, Grandpa heard a name he knew, and Jackson read the whole listing. Today he didn't recognize anybody.

He struggled with his coffee lid. "Hate these damn squishy

Styrofoam cups."

Jackson knew he wouldn't ask for help. And since Jackson was feeling particularly black this morning, he didn't offer any. The lid finally came off and Grandpa Pedro took a long, loud slurp.

He wrinkled his nose. "That fancy stuff?"

"That's what I like."

"Waste a'money. What you pay, three dollars for these coffees? I never paid more than a dime in my life."

"And you still haven't. I have. You're welcome."

"Dinner made me sick again last night," his grandfather growled. "Beginning to think the problem is me. Might not be around much longer, you know. At my age, really, I could go any minute."

"Only the young die good," Jackson mumbled.

"What's that?"

"Nothing."

Grandpa Pedro stared out the window. "Yup, dinner was downright lousy. The nurse asked me how I liked it, I told her it looked like something that the dog threw up." He continued like this. Somehow the nurses found it endearing.

Jackson stopped listening. He reflexively uhm-hmmed when pauses prompted him to do so, frowned when his grandfather's tone became especially harsh. But he was thinking about his wrist, wondering if he should have it looked at. It hurt, but it wasn't swollen. Wouldn't it swell if he'd broken it?

This morning? No. Last night. Evening, really. After the red-bikini girl had left, Jackson went to the Sunset Restaurant. The Sunset used to be the Gray Whale, a place frequented (and therefore made a popular tourist destination) by Jared Ferryman. Why did everything in L.A. smack of Jackson's alter ego?

The Sunset served painfully mediocre food dressed up in

fancy sauces and served with flower-cut radishes and bunny-folded napkins. But the wait staff smiled and laughed with him, and at five, the piano bar opened. Like the restaurant, the singer proved comfortably predictable: in tune, mid-range versions of Billy Joel and Beatles songs designed to leave the Malibu barflies nostalgic. The atmosphere and a bottle of wine kept him warmly buzzed until the sun left only a line of violet against the black horizon of the sea.

A few songs and cups of coffee later, Jackson had headed out. The walk up the beachway seemed longer in the dark, and cars lined it only intermittently now. Toward the end, where the beach-front road met the PCH, Jackson heard a nasty argument.

"You. Backed. Over. My. Bike!" A young man's voice.

Jackson stopped in the shadows. "My bike" referred to a small bright green Honda lying next to the kid, sideways and dented. The kid, tall but thin, faced off against three well-built older looking guys whose surfboard-filled Land Rover had apparently backed over Slim's motorcycle. Slim wanted insurance info.

He wasn't getting it. "If you had a real bike instead of that Jap piece of shit, maybe it could handle a little love tap."

It always eluded Jackson when people in real life behaved the way of people on television. He searched the ground and found a piece of driftwood to serve as a big stick, then without moving from the shadows said calmly, "Give him your insurance numbers and get off my beach."

The bullies acted according to script, playing nice cop/nasty cop, with two of them talking tough while getting in the truck to leave. But the nasty one had some point to prove, and lumbered at Jackson frothing obscenities. CRACK! and the driftwood busted in two over Nasty's head.

The friends rushed after him, spewing curse-spangled

information. "I was fucking getting it, dude. I'm with Triple A, fuck! You didn't have to break his goddamn head open, he's just drunk . . ." The driver tossed a AAA business card at Jackson, then he and the other nice guy loaded their friend into the truck. They sped off with a grind of rubber and a flume of sand.

Slim propped his bike up, but it practically formed a V— clearly unrideable.

"You need a lift?" Jackson offered.

"Naw, I called somebody." He sounded more frightened than before.

Jackson saw the glow of a cell phone and figured the kid would be fine. He handed him the insurance card, then fought déjà vu the rest of his way home. Back at his hotbox apartment, the adrenaline must finally have faded, since his hand started throbbing. This morning its ache had woken him up. But no swelling. And no health insurance. Probably it was fine, right?

A sing-songy voice tore through his reverie. "Sailor Man! Breakfast is ready!"

Grampa Pedro cringed as he always did at her effervescence. But instead of resigning himself to being wheeled down to the dining room, he suddenly turned on Jackson with the previous day's lucidity. "Why do you work anyway, kid?"

Jackson somehow managed to keep his mouth from falling open. "Uhh . . . what?"

"Didn't you make enough money being famous? What are you working for?" The old man leaned in, his eyes glowing with concern. "Is it because you're back in L.A.? Too expensive here?"

Jackson stared stupidly at a man he'd thought he knew.

"Um . . ." All this time he'd been lying and he could have been telling the truth? "I thought you'd want me to work."

Grampa Pedro's wrinkled face absolutely pruned with confusion. "WHY? Why work if you don't have to?"

"I'll, uh . . . quit. If you'd like?"

"It's about what you'd like." A bony finger stuck Jackson in the chest.

The same sickeningly cheerful nurse appeared in the doorway again. "Mister Sailor's going to be late. Don't want cold eggs. Not yummy."

Jackson assured her they'd be right down.

His grandfather wagged a finger after the nurse. "It's about what you'd like," he said, "with one exception." He gazed at Jackson, his eyes glowing with an immediacy the younger man did not recognize. "When was I in the Navy, kid?"

"During the war?"

"Right. I was drafted into World War II along with most of the rest of the world. And that's when I happened to meet your grandmother. Her parents wanted her with a Marine, not a sailor. She told them I'd proposed. They said, Not that sailor! Her father called me Mister Sailor until the day he dropped dead. Four years in the Navy, no more. But guess what your grandmother made me promise to put on my tombstone?" Affection stippled his voice.

"It's about what'd you'd like," he continued, "except for the way you're introduced to the world. That's a big truth, that introduction. Even if it's wrong! Even if it's wrong, it's a big, wild, crazy truth. Because it's how others see you. And people's opinions are their truths. Their reality."

Jackson gaped at his grandfather. When was the last time they'd spoken like this? Jackson had still been in high school. He wanted to keep it going. "What if their reality doesn't match yours? What do you do?"

Grampa Pedro shrugged. "What I did was I fought against all my life. I could have re-enlisted. Should have. Millie wouldda been happier. But I fought it. You can fight it or you can embrace it. Either way, it's gonna come find you in the end."

Grampa Pedro stared past him, into something Jackson wasn't privy to, maybe his warm past with Gramma Millie? Maybe his cold, dark future in the ground. Jackson, meanwhile, considered Melvina. She was certainly fighting her introduction to the world. Unapologetically! But Grampa was right, that fighting came at a price.

Jackson realized that Melina knew this, was well aware, that when she'd winked at him while they'd been refilling the crayon, it was a literal wink-and-nod, really acknowledging not sexism, but a different prejudice. The kind you experience when the world says you're that but you know you're this.

"Wouldn't it be easier to just find people who agreed with you?" he asked his grandfather.

The old man looked at him curiously, as if he wasn't confident about the context of the question. A pang of loss flitted through Jackson.

And what was he? Jackson? Other than a washed-up TV actor slowly slipping into obscurity in a crappy apartment in North Hollywood? Doing a poor, impatient job of helping an old man die. Just what would Jackson Blake be fighting for?

As Jackson wondered this, he watched his grandfather's face slip from alert and alive back to dull and droopy. From his jaunty, curious grandfather whom he admired, to a sick, elderly man he felt sorry for.

The old man faced him. "Hey, we'd better get down there! I don't want cold eggs. That slop is bad enough warm."

* * *

"Don't you have anything smaller?"

Jackson blinked at the clerk and the hundred dollar bill he'd handed him, then fumbled with the wallet. "I, uh . . . I dunno."

Had the kid behind the counter been less uninterested, he might have noticed the streaky fingerprints on the black leather wallet, smears of crimson that would dry to brown by dawn. But at 4:30 in the morning, Quick Mart clerks have more pressing concerns than a confused, subtly blood-stained man unfamiliar with his monies.

Jackson dug through the stranger's wallet, found a twenty and took the C-note back from the clerk. He collected his newspaper, two unfancy Grampa coffees, and box of donuts. He got back in his car, headed to the nursing home, and the entire event went unremarked.

At a long stoplight, he flipped through the wallet to find out whose it was, maybe get it back to them. Ed Bloodworth, the guy in the driver's license photo, looked surprisingly decent. And young, especially for his Melrose address. Probably worked in the industry. Had a nice face—broad and high-cheekboned, big blue eyes against pale skin, and a red wave of hair. And this was a license photo. Whose license photo looked that good?

Jackson had pulled into the convenience store lot just as the young man exited his souped-up 1969 Mustang. Primer gray but the engine purred. The kid made the mistake of parking his muscle car in front of the store but out of the light. So he didn't see the guy in the dark alley along the side of the building. The guy who pointed a gun at him and dragged him in to the darkness.

On whatever death-wish whim, Jackson followed, found a second robber back there, a thin wiry shadow. The shadow cackled profanity-riddled insults at the Mustang kid, who lay on the ground, silent, taking a beating.

"Police!" Jackson bellowed, flashing open his wallet in hopes of maybe faking himself some clout.

Wirey cursed and fled.

"Pinche puto!" the gun-guy yelled after him in an accent

that told Jackson he was white. The he turned to Jackson. "You're no fucking cop!" He displayed a mouth full of teeth. "But since you're back here, pendajo, what you got? Huh? Hand it over!"

The gun gleamed and its owner came at Jackson like a late train. Jackson heard the injured man stir and whimper from behind the dumpster. A pitiful, distressing sound that awoke in Jackson a righteous bravery. *Always help the helpless . . .*

Everything slowed and made sense.

Jackson landed a solid foot to the gunman's groin with his steel-toed engineer's boots. The perp fell like a sack of manure, and the gun skittered away. Jackson caught sight of the victim limping off, a dark hunch against the blossoming daylight. He kicked the robber in the face, heard a groan. He stomped on one of his hands, then snatched the gun from the ground and turned it against perp. "Consider your ticket punched," he growled.

But he didn't shoot. The robber was already knocked out and had pissed himself either from injury or out of fear. Jackson pointed the gun at him, curious if he could pull the trigger under the right circumstances. But these weren't them. That fact pulled him back to broader reality. He'd retrieved the Mustang kid's wallet from the alley, taken a moment to not puke by the dumpster, then gone in the store like nothing had happened.

Now he pulled into the nursing home parking lot nearly fifteen minutes late. The elevator seemed to take forever and when it finally did open on the third floor, Grampa Pedro wasn't waiting. Just an empty lobby full of oppressive furniture and plastic flowers.

Jackson headed to his grandfather's room, imagining the lecture he'd be subjected to this morning. Maybe the donuts would shield him. Yeah, they could be his excuse. They didn't have the right ones at—

Halfway down the hall Jackson noticed something different.

It seemed smaller somehow. The doors were all closed, that was it. So someone had died. And here came the nurse, her face a portrait of sympathy, so Jackson knew it was his someone.

"We're so sorry . . . in his sleep . . . tried to phone you . . . wish to see the body?"

See the body? Good lord no!

"The body is a husk," he mumbled, and got back on the elevator.

It smelled like cigars and leather again—like the Perfumed Woman. The gun weighted Jackson's pocket in a hauntingly familiar way. The sensation of its weight combined with that tantalizing scent to form a forceful elixir. It solidified his sense of completion. It washed away the creeping guilt of not being too mournful about losing Grampa Pedro, of feeling his grandfather had been gone a long time already.

Jackson left the nursing home feeling content and confident, like he finally fit into the world. And why not?

Jared Ferryman didn't have any living relatives.

The Ocean Doesn't Want Me Today

Because Buffalo had burned them out, not with its weather but through its economic dilapidation, and because they had visited Cambridge multiple times and had a good time every time, cousins Eva and Madeline Drinkwater decided to move to Boston that summer. But months of careful if nervous planning could not overcome fate, and seven days before their scheduled departure, Uncle Emerson called them up to Maine.

Emerson Drinkwater represented Favorite Eccentric Uncle and last of the Drinkwater Lobstermen. The latter doubtlessly contributed to the former, but only in a sublime sense. "These lobstaw licenses are a hawd find," he drawled. Maine-iac, their grandmother had called him. "Once you give it up, it's out of the family for good. I . . . am an old man."

His statement, as they stood rooting through purses and duffels for brushes and oil wipes after fifteen hours in the car, broadsided them. The cousins stopped their fussing and came to rest in chairs across the kitchen table from him. It was the same table they remembered from summer visits as children, white enamel with a pull-out leaf. Eva's now-adult eye realized the value of this Art Deco original. She sipped lemonade—homemade, she noted—from a Mason jar. "But we're city girls."

Uncle Emerson lit an enormous white pipe. He stood six-four, and his wiry, silver beard stopped at his navel, a part seemingly on display given his open short-sleeve denim shirt and modest Buddha belly. He wore his hair in a hoary braid reminiscent of a rope. Even confined, it came to his waist.

Eyes like lit coal, Gramma always said of him. Madeline squirmed beneath his gaze, attempted to sit cross-legged—Indian style—on the smallish wooden chair.

Emerson's burning eyes hooded slightly. His finger pointed, hovered, decided on Eva. "You—spent a summer as a cull girl."

"One summer. I was maybe thirteen."

"No. It was ten years back. You were sixteen."

"I was thirteen that summer," said Madeline, "but they wouldn't let me on the boat."

She was answered by being ignored. So she sulked in the nighttime gloom of the kitchen. It still smelled of the same warm spices Emerson's wife, Aunt Stella, had worked magic with. The tough, sweet lady had been dead almost two years now.

In the living room, the same afghan hung over the back of the brown plaid couch. Stella's purple rocking chair still clashed with everything else in the house, though it seemed empty without her big tabby cat, Moxie. The scent of cinnamon potpourri continued to cling to the living room, and lilac drifted in from the backyard.

Outside, even at this late hour, the sun maintained enough presence to stain the sky deep purple and violent red. In the silence, if Madeline held her breath, she could hear the distant, rhythmic rush of the ocean. She sensed as well a faraway peace, just out of reach, like the waves.

Later, the cousins lay sprawled across twin beds which had

belonged to Emerson's sons, Ash and Rowan. ("He wanted to call them Hunter and Hemingway," Gramma told the girls, over and over the way old people do. "Hunter Drinkwater? Can you imagine! Thank God Stella had some sense!") The boys had set out from this navy blue room with its matching pinewood beds and footlockers to become a dental hygienist and a high-school chemistry teacher, respectively.

"No AC," Eva moaned.

"It's not that hot."

"It's humid."

"And you want to live in Boston?"

"In Boston, people are civilized. They condition the air." Eva kicked off the sheet. "This room seems smaller. The whole house does."

"That's because we're bigger."

"I also remember it being more fun here."

"It was, when the boys were still here."

"They were hardly boys. Rowan is what, thirty-two now?"

Madeline did some quick math. "Yeah. Ash is thirty-five." It struck her that her father was closer in age to his nephews—Emerson's boys—than he was to Emerson—his brother. But Eva didn't like to talk about Madeline's father, so Madeline didn't point this out, instead asking, "So when they hung with us, they were college kids?"

"Grad students," Eva answered.

"That was nice of them."

"College boys love high school girls," Eva said. "We're supposed to call Ash, by the way. He says he found us an apartment for next month. "

"But next month starts next week."

"So?"

"What if we're not ready by then?"

"Ready?"

"To leave."

"What is it you want to do, Maddy? One day in Bar Harbor and you've seen it all. We're not rich folk with endless supplies of boating entertainment."

"Maybe I want to hunt lobsters."

Eva laughed. When Madeline didn't, Eva stopped. "You mean it."

"Yeah? What if I do?"

Eva let out an irritated sigh. "You don't want to be a lobsterman. It's a backbreaking, smelly job that would require you to live here."

"It's beautiful here."

"In the summer. As a tourist. Think snow, Maddy. Snow and a boat? People die. Add incredibly dangerous to the list."

Madeline, still under her sheet, flopped over on her side. The bedrooms were nestled in the eaves of the little cape house, and the dormers faced the ocean. She couldn't hear it now, though, not over the fan.

"I'd just like to try it," she admitted. "You know, for size or whatever. See if it fits."

"You're crazy." Eva told her around a yawn.

"Don't you find it romantic?"

"Not at all. So, not to be cruel, but I suggest you get real. Because he won't give you the business, just us."

"Or you," Madeline mumbled. Eva responded, but Madeline ignored her, pretended to be asleep. Shortly the hum of the fan and the distant rhythm of the ocean—which she swore she could feel even if she couldn't hear it—soon these things led her to slumber.

* * *

The warm buttery scent of pancakes overrode the iodine tang of the sea, waking the girls in the morning. Madeline headed down. Eva told her she wanted to shower first.

"You just showered before you went to bed."

"But I sweated all last night."

As Maddy entered the kitchen, the screen door banged closed, and from outside a bowed, diminutive man called out a rusty goodbye.

"I didn't mean to chase away your company," she said.

Emerson set a cup of coffee in front of her. "Old fisherman friend," he told her. "Getting a late start this morning, stopped in for coffee."

Emerson had made buttermilk pancakes, topped with blueberries and dusted with powdered sugar. By the time Eva made it down, hers were cold. Emerson dug a microwave from out of a closet. "Your aunt used this. I can't stand them. Give you tumors or something."

"What about for heating coffee?"

"Room temperature is good enough."

A knock at the front door startled the girls. Emerson let out a soft sigh, not bothering to answer or even call out that it was open, before it swung wide and Rowan whirled in.

"Hey Daddy! Did you get my message?"

"Yes."

"Oh. I didn't think you'd be home. I mean, I can show the girls around. If you need to go to work or whatever."

"They're not here to be shown around. They're here to learn the business and decide if they want it."

"Oh, no." He turned to the girls, both at the table. "I thought you were kidding." He took a seat, stabbed at one of

Eva's pancakes. "These are good!"

"Your dad made them."

"Trying to butter the girls up, Dad?"

Emerson stared at him blankly.

"No pun intended," said Rowan. "I didn't think Eva was serious in her email. She told me you called them up here. I figured she was being funny and they were just on vacation."

"Yeah? And . . . ?"

Rowan sighed in a way that mimicked his father's earlier. His voice was sympathetic. "Daddy, it's a dying art, what you do. We didn't want the business either."

"She hasn't been on a boat yet."

"Kind of my point. She hasn't been on a boat ever in her life."

Eva corrected this statement. Emerson used the resulting gleeful argument to shield his escape. Watching him go, Madeline felt both sorry for and angry at him.

Rowan's feelings apparently mirrored hers. "Poor Dad," he said, shaking his head. "It just sticks in his craw to think he may have to retire."

Eva frowned. "Just how will dragging us up here remedy his retirement issue?"

"He didn't drag us," Madeline said. "We could have said no."

Rowan answered Eva's question: "If he can hand the business over to someone in the family, then he'll have to teach us how to run it, right? But if the licenses go to another family, well, they won't need him. He'll be stuck on shore."

Madeline thought, but did not tell her cousins, that being run ashore would kill her uncle. Before she'd been offered a say, Eva informed her that the three of them, Eva, Rowan and Madeline, would be spending the day "on the island"—meaning

Mount Desert Island. Meaning, really, Bar Harbor.

Outside, Madeline was struck by beauty most places can only produce the morning after a violent rainstorm. Pine trees invade the beaches in Maine, and today they stood verdant against a deep blue sky dotted with cotton-ball clouds.

Like a painting, Madeline thought. What a contrast to Buffalo's hazy orange summer skies. More like San Diego, where she'd lived before. But where San Diego was bridled beauty and Buffalo dying and industry-choked, Maine was untamed, seemingly untamable.

"So why are you not working today?" she asked Rowan on the drive.

"I'm off for the summer. Best three things about being a teacher, right? June, July and August." He winked at her in the rearview. "Actually, I usually teach summer school. But I'd planned to go to Paris this summer."

"What happened?"

"With Iraq and the war, I decided against it."

Eva, in the passenger's seat, elbowed him.

"Anyway," he continued, "now I get to spend the summer hanging out with you guys. When's the last time we did that?"

"We were just talking about that last night, how summers were more fun with you and Ash."

"Here's Park Loop Road. How about hiking?"

Eva rolled her eyes. "Do I appear to be dressed for hiking?"

Rowan glanced at her hound's-tooth capris and tie-back halter.

"For that matter," Eva said, "neither are you."

Rowan waved a hand. "Eddie Bauer—good for all activities."

"Oh really? So you're always prepared, are you? Like James Bond?"

"Exactly like James Bond. Or, you know, a Boy Scout."

In town they wandered hilly streets, pawed over tourist trinkets and the occasional true work of art. Eva bought a sweatshirt and some assorted lighthouse-themed kitsch "For our new place."

Rowan wanted ice cream. Eva refused. "I'm trying to lose weight."

"For fifteen hours," Madeline scoffed, "you ate nothing but beef jerky, Gatorade and McDonalds."

"All the more reason to be careful now." To Rowan, she explained: "Food choices on the road are limited."

He answered in earnest. "Hopefully we can find you a suitable place for dinner."

He and Madeline got ice cream.

Later, Eva loitered outside the chocolate shop while Madeline and Rowan oohed and aahed, finally settling on two giant truffles to split and share: one hazelnut and one apricot.

"Eva's like the vacation police," Rowan said inside.

"She's putting on airs," Madeline assured him. "We had a great time on the drive up." She sampled his truffle, raved about it. "Besides, she means well. My dad says she can't help it; this is how her mother acts and that's what women do." She smiled.

"Do you, uh . . . hear much from your dad?"

"Yeah. He writes at least once a week. What's funny is sometimes the letters come in big bunches, a month's worth at a time. I like to open just one a day. You know he—"

Sharp tapping on the glass shut her up. Eva gestured to her wrist, to a watch that wasn't there, as if they were on a schedule. Back outside, Madeline suggested a whale watch, but her cousins pretended not to hear her. Still, it is nearly impossible not to get near the ocean in Bar Harbor, and Eva seemed to figure this out around three o'clock. "Maybe we could go hiking. I like the carriage trails."

"If we're going hiking, I need food." Rowan started across the street to Epi's, a pizza joint favored by the locals because it stayed open all year round.

The girls gaped at each other. "He's bottomless," said Eva.

They trailed after him, Madeline leading. "It's hardly hiking. The trails are wider than these streets, and everything is flat."

"Is it outside?" Rowan countered, laughing.

"Yes."

"Is it paved?"

"No. But there's—"

"Then it's hiking."

"It's walking."

"It's hiking."

Rowan purchased and consumed two slices of pepperoni pizza, and then the three of them headed to the carriage trails.

Just after five, the mosquitoes rained down on them like a plague. Eva quit after being bitten twice and noticing the undulating web of black that had settled on Rowan's beige shirt. She fled to the car. "How do people live here?" Rowan and Madeline made a show of trying to prove to each other how tough they were, but the buzzing, like a distant chainsaw, eventually sent them running as well, back to the safety of Rowan's silver Toyota.

"Return to civilization?" Rowan asked.

"How about the quiet side of the island?" Madeline suggested. "There must be someplace there to eat."

He put the car in gear and moseyed back onto the main road. "Driving Miss Madeline."

"That's what I need," said Eva, dreamily. "A chauffer. I could roll out of bed and into the car, then get ready on the way to work."

"You do that now."

"You're funny, Maddy. You should take that act on the road. Don't worry, I won't forget the little people. When I'm a partner, with a corner office and a brass name—why are you turning here?"

"I thought we'd hit the beach quick," Rowan answered. "That way we won't be smelly at the restaurant." He grinned.

"I don't think the beach is such a good idea." She swung her eyes to Madeline.

Madeline flicked her cousin's ear. "I want to go to the beach."

Rowan smiled at her. "Two against one, Eva."

She glared at him, but they did indeed go to the beach—one of two in the area with sand and not just rocks (the sand imported from someplace else.) A sign at the entranceway informed then that the water was fifty-two degrees today, that the typical high for the summer was fifty-eight, and the record was a whopping sixty-two.

A few kids splashed around in the water. Rowan went in to his ankles, came out covered in goosebumps. Eva stood on the beach examining her nails and sighing. Madeline dipped a toe in. It felt to her like setting foot in a glass of ice water. She rushed in up to her knees, to the cuff of her rolled-up jeans, and let out a scream along with the kids in the water. They all giggled together. She wondered what it must feel like to swim the English Channel, or jump through cut ice like the Polar Bear Club. She wondered about how the riptide would feel if it caught her—was it peaceful like they promise? When her mother's lungs filled with water, had she finally, with grace and thanks, given in?

She walked deeper into the waves. The icy water wicked up her shorts, made her gasp. She ducked her head below the next wave and swam under it. Beneath, the water was strangely still, no violent currents to whisk her away. She bobbed back to the surface, had to swim a good ten yards in before her feet could again touch bottom.

Back on the beach, she watched Eva giggle at everything Rowan said, screech when he splashed her, and finally throw sand at him. Sand. Where Madeline's father was, that's all they had. She thought about her father, her hero, reduced to numbers on a chain by his government—his job—and to nudges and whispers by his family. In town they'd seen many signs, "Support Our Troops, Bring Them Home." Support my Dad, Madeline thought. Talk about him.

"Maddy!" Rowan called. "We're hungry." Then he saw her. "Christ, you're soaked."

"What's the matter with you?" Eva asked as Madeline trundled back to the shore. "You knew we were going out. You expect us to drive all the way back to Emerson's now? You know there's no place to eat in Ellsworth."

Madeline stood, dripping and panting. "What?"

"It's fine," said Rowan, "Her shirt will dry, and I have a pair of swim trunks in the car." He winked at Madeline again. "You can roll the waistband down to your hips like those sorority girls."

"Just so long as there's no letters printed on the ass."

"Like what?" asked Eva. "This space for rent?"

Madeline shimmied out of her wet jeans and into Rowan's trunks in the backseat of the car. She nimbly avoided any conversations about where to eat, other than to remind her cousins that she had a limited budget.

"My treat," Rowan insisted.

"In that case, how about the Blue Mosquito?"

She'd been kidding, but Rowan agreed with alacrity. "I've always wanted to try it there and Daddy refused!"

* * *

The Blue Mosquito looked, superficially, like a salty old fisherman's hangout. Two stories of driftwood tables and ship's wheel chandeliers, housed in a white-washed wharf house. The menu, however, belied this image, listing gourmet grub at connoisseur cost. The wine list came in at ten pages, bottles only, nothing offered by the glass.

Three glasses of wine each on an empty stomach left both girls giddy. Rowan smartly designated himself the driver and stopped after one, sipping sparkling water instead.

"How fancy," Eva noted.

"When in Rome . . ."

Madeline grinned. "When in Sane . . ."

"You would know," mumbled Eva.

"I'm sorry, am I interrupting your day-long attempt to seduce your first cousin?"

Rowan reddened. "I think we could use some bread. Where is that waiter?"

Eva waved a finger. "You're disgusting. And this is precisely what I meant. You say things that don't make any sense."

"How would you even know? You never listen."

"Never listen? I've been listening to you for over a decade!"

People glanced at their table. Rowan leaned in slightly. "Really ladies, there's no need to fight. I mean, it's not like your sisters or anything."

"That's exactly what it's like," Eva said, "and that's the problem. Thirteen years as an only child, and suddenly I inherit a half-orphaned sister."

Eva broke into her well-practiced litany. How she didn't have the preparative warning of a pregnancy or get a cute, round baby sister, just some preteen to hand her clothes down to. Just competition. In sports, in grades, in boys.

"You know what?" Madeline snapped. "It sucked for me, too."

"At least you were used to sharing things and not always getting what you wanted. Your parents were poor." The word came off Eva's tongue like an olive pit.

"Being a soldier doesn't pay well. Write your congressman."

"Daddy was poor," Rowan said. "There's not buckets of money in those lobster traps, you know." He poked Eva in the ribs. "I'd say your father was the exception in this family, kiddo."

"Well, he was the first to go to college. But it's good that your dad took over the family legacy. Someone should have. As for Uncle Errol," her eyes lit on Madeline, "You have to admit it might have helped if they'd waited to have a kid until they had some money."

Madeline's eyes hooded. "Condoms break. You know that."

Eva reddened only slightly. "Of course, Gramma was over forty when she had your father."

"So? So what!"

"So your father was obviously an accident himself. He's lucky he's not IQ 80. Happens a lot with those last babies. Yet another piece of baggage you came with. I hate to be the one to tell you this, but we are tired of having to walk on eggshells for you."

Madeline looked hard into her cousin's contorted face. "You honestly believe that, don't you?"

"What?"

"You have twisted this . . . act of yours into something I need. You think you're some kind of martyr or something. Oh, poor Maddy needs to be protected. Don't talk about the war. Don't let her on a boat. That's how it's always been. From you and your horrible parents."

Eva stood. "You call my parents horrible?"

Rowan hushed her gently, tried to get her to sit. She ignored him.

"After they agreed to take you in so your useless father could stay in the Marines? Even Gramma says it's the only place he's fit to work."

"The Marines are exclusive."

"—And he certainly picked himself a real winner of a wife—"

Maddy leapt to her feet, knocking her chair over. "You shut up!"

"—in your over-indulged, artsy-fartsy mother who killed herself!"

Rowan's mouth fell open. The restaurant seemed to go quiet. Eva crossed her arms, smiling with the crooked pride of someone who has stung somebody to the quick.

But Madeline had the trump card. "I know she did."

"You do?" It was Rowan who asked.

Madeline shook her head at him. "You disappoint me. Her, I expect it from."

"What the hell is that supposed to mean?" Eva snapped.

"My mother sent me a letter. She mailed it the day she drowned herself. Very artsy-fartsy. 'If you're reading this, then I haven't intercepted it from you, and the ocean wanted me this time.'"

"How come you never told us?" Rowan asked.

"Nobody wanted to hear it."

Eva snorted. "Bullshit. You enjoyed the attention."

"Horseshit! You—and your parents—need me to be breakable. Need an excuse to not talk about it, to lie to the school and the neighbors about why they suddenly have a spare kid. 'Boating accident.' Lots more acceptable at the country club and cocktail hour than 'Her mom killed herself.'"

Eva, for once, remained silent. She fell loosely into her chair. Rowan retrieved Madeline's for her and she eased into it, thanking him. She felt no satisfaction.

Eva's argument was true—Madeline had enjoyed the attention. At first. She got the letter and read it and hid it, afraid that if her Aunts and Uncles knew the truth, no one would let her stay with them, think she was tainted or something. October replaced July, and she moved from San Diego to Buffalo.

Eventually she figured out that they knew the truth, but they thought she didn't. An opportunity never presented itself for her to set them straight. The more time that passed, the less able she felt able to tell, like having known a person too long to possibly inquire their name.

The waiter appeared, bread basket in hand. "Will you be staying, then?" he asked without irony or alarm. He smiled around the table in a way that said he'd seen far worse and not to worry.

"Yes," Rowan told him. "We're staying. Thank you."

The bread was warm and sweet. The salads were full of odd, tasty greens Madeline had never seen before, and the escargot she ordered melted in her mouth and made the rest of the wine taste like honey.

Eva suggested to Madeline that they split dessert—her small, immediate way of apologizing. Later, Madeline knew, she'd be more forthright. She noticed that Eva's chatter with Rowan had cooled slightly, become less enthusiastic and more adult, and a pang of regret sat heavy in her chest. Well, no retraction was possible now. Besides, they got on the topics of Ash's children, and how Gramma was living with Ash but should probably be in a home, and the girls' plans once they got to Boston. Things that should be discussed, things with gravity and ramifications and consequences.

Madeline kept reticent. Letting Eva speak for both of them allowed her distance from them, for her mind mulled something less immediate but more looming.

There were times when she'd believed the euphemism her family had designed, that her mother's death had been an accident, that Mom hadn't meant to leave—what kind of parent abandons her only child? But Madeline knew the answer to that, too. From the same source, read and re-read with understanding that increased with her age.

By not telling them about the letter, Madeline had encouraged her family to lie to her for a decade. She'd dug her own hole, and now had to crawl out of it.

* * *

Madeline woke up cold. She'd kicked off all her covers, and Eva had apparently stolen them, since she now lay in peaceful slumber, wrapped in three layers of blanket. Madeline snapped the fan off, spooked herself with the sudden silence. Maybe there were more blankets in the hall closet.

The way to the linen cupboard brought her past the bathroom, which seemed awfully bright. She peered in, discerned that the light came from outside, and pushed the plastic curtain from the window.

The moon hung in the sky like a lit nickel. Perfectly round and glowing; she could have read by it. The previous day's clouds stretched out around it like black pillows in the ink blue sky. Madeline distinguished five different birds chirping and twittering from the yard below. Night birds? Or did the brightness of the moon confuse them? She wondered what time it was.

She padded downstairs. By the time she'd crept out the backdoor, the moon had slid behind a veil of clouds. The sky around it glowed navy now, tattling dawn's arrival.

How long since she'd seen a summer sunrise? Since the summer her mom died. She remembered how, at age thirteen, watching the sun come up after being up all night had seemed to her like watching the Earth reform itself each morning: amorphous shadows forged into solid, familiar forms.

A truck rattled by. Madeline held her breath, heard heavy bells and distant yelling. Fishermen saw this every morning. Did it become unremarkable? Nothing had ever become unremarkable to Madeline's mother. Even when her eyesight first began to fail, she'd claimed it made the world "more interesting."

"How long have you known about your muhthaw?" Emerson's slow drawl interrupted but did not startle her.

"Since three days after."

She heard her Uncle breathe slow and deliberate in the budding morning.

"For my mom," she said, "her work—her painting—was her life. Her blindness put her out of work."

Emerson's lit his pipe. "Get ready," he said. "Be quick."

She scuttled upstairs, pulled on her rolled-up jeans from yesterday and a tank top, and grabbed her ragged red sweatshirt to wear until the sun brought its heat. Her short hair couldn't be tamed quickly or without a hairdryer, so she yanked on her tank cap, a green watch cap with a brim, like Radar from M*A*S*H wore.

"A gift from your father," Emerson observed. He walked through the arbor, once lined with roses but bare now that Aunt Stella was gone. Like she took them with her, Rowan had told them. The yellow flowers had threatened to conquer the entire yard, then the summer after Stella died, they didn't come back.

From the road, half the sky glowed like midmorning, while the east still hid in murky dawn.

"Errol—Dad, to you—once told me that he joined the Marines so he could see the sunrise."

"He told me it was because he wanted to feel like part of something."

Emerson slowed, glanced over his shoulder. His face sort of crumpled, almost imperceptibly, so Madeline wondered if she'd enlightened her uncle, and if the knowledge wounded him.

No answer came through in his voice. "There's twenty one years between me and Errol. Nineteen between him and your uncle Brodie." He gazed at her pointedly. "I did ask Errol to join me on the boat."

"I know you did. He didn't want to. Says the ocean scares him. That's why he joined the Marines, not the Navy."

"Scares me too. That's why I became a lobsterman."

They traipsed down a gravel road lined with cottages. Outside one of them, a woman watered a lush garden. Emerson waved in silent greeting. Farther up, a huge but slender orange cat sat in the open window of an A-frame house, watching wide-eyed as birds awakened and chittered at each other. Mountains appeared, stained purple in the off light. Emerson led the way through a clearing and a road materialized, thin but paved.

He pointed right. "About two miles. Third dock. There's a red boat and a man named Rusty. You met him yesterday—he's the one came for coffee." Emerson gave a loose salute and headed left. Over his shoulder he called, "We'll talk at dinner."

She found the dock and the red boat. She'd forgotten about the incredible disparity between high and low tides Downeast, and was at first puzzled by the distance between the dock and the boat, united by a worn-slick rope ladder.

She'd expected something large in the way of boats, with a wheelhouse, a big rudder and an engine you couldn't see. The wee widget in the water looked like a broad rowboat and had an outboard motor, currently angled out of the water. An orange-and white-striped buoy stood at an angle, nailed to the rim on the starboard side.

Looking around for Rusty, Madeline caught sight of a man in the distance, up the road opposite from the side she'd come, a slightly stooped man dressed in bright yellow coveralls over a denim shirt. He waved like he'd been expecting her. As he got closer, she saw that the overalls were waterproof, along with the black galoshes that went nearly up to the petite man's knees.

Rusty's moniker referred not to his coloring—wind and salt had tanned his loose skin to almond, and what was left of his hair matched his boots—but his voice, which Madeline did recognize from the previous morning, a labored creak he forced from his throat with incongruent cheer. "Sorry I'm late," he brayed. "I had to cram an owl into my freezer."

Madeline shook her head. "Owl?"

"Yeah, it was circling my place, so I shot him. I'm gonna stuff him. That's what I do. See?" A wallet materialized and Madeline found herself dazed by a series of glossy photos of taxidermied fish and fowl, tucked into the plastic flaps where pictures of grandchildren typically are housed.

"I got a lynx, too, somebody gave me. Friend of mine works with parks and rec. But I'm not so good with fur just yet. Anyway, you ever been on a boat before?"

"Not really."

"It's not so hard. The ones they use, the business lobster fishing boats? Those are decked out with radar, depth sounders, CBs, radios . . . Even stuff I never heard of—GPS?"

"Global positioning systems?"

"Yeah. All computerized. Pretty amazing."

"Do you work with my uncle?"

"Naw, we're friends. I got my own traps. You know the

state lets everybody put some out. But we gotta stick to the same rules as the big guys, so Emerson figures I can teach you the basics, I guess."

Rusty slithered down the ladder and into the boat. He pulled keys from his pocket, found a small one, and unlocked the cabinet taking up the back three feet of the boat.

Madeline made her way down the rope ladder: cold and wet in her hands but comfortable, familiar. She stepped to the boat, felt herself breathe when she didn't tip it over. Wanting to maintain that relief, she immediately sat on the thin bench in the center.

Now that she sat in it, the boat seemed bigger. Two wooden traps, the old half-round style, rested by the cabinet, one on either side of where Rusty stood rummaging. Their wood had silvered with age and wear, lending them a stoic beauty. Madeline located a gas can, a pickle bucket, a blanket. The more she looked the more she saw. What did the cabinet hold?

Rusty stuck a life jacket on her. "Emerson said to keep you out of the water. What's the matter, you don't swim good?"

"I swim great. My family thinks I may try to kill myself, is the problem."

"Oh. Yeah?" He seemed to be sizing her up. "Well it ain't legal to stuff people, so don't worry. I won't push ya!"

She laughed, despite her chagrin.

He donned an orange vest himself, reached under the lip of the boat and produced a pair of oars. "We'll ride this out to the bay. I got one trap in here, two out in the bay."

He rowed slowly for maybe a mile, pointing out stuff along the coast and telling her the rules of lobstering. "Can't take 'em too big or too little. Gotta show your license at all times, along with your colors." He gestured to the mounted buoy. "There's only certain months when you really lobster, when you're really out on the boat, right? Rest of the time is spent doin' paperwork and fixing your gear."

"My cousin says it's dangerous. Especially in the winter."

"Biggest danger on the boat is prob'ly the ropes."

When Rusty didn't elaborate, Madeline asked, "What happens?"

"You get tangled up, you go down with the traps, you get yourself dead. Here we are." He stopped rowing and pointed to the mouth of the river. To the side, a buoy matching Rusty's bobbed in the current.

From the opposite lip where he'd obtained the oars, Rusty now unearthed a hooked pole. He snagged the buoy and grabbed its spindle.

"You pull them up by hand?" Madeline asked.

"Yep. I do. Not the commercial guys, not anymore. Your uncle's boat, that's got electric winches."

He said more but Madeline didn't listen. "What is that noise?" The air had filled with a sound like a whining dog, or a whistling seagull.

"Looky there." Rusty pointed the buoy over her head to a tree full of fat dots.

Birds sat, maybe a dozen, manifest in a tree ripe with buds but still no foliage. Even from the distance, the birds were large enough that Madeline could easily distinguish their chocolate brown bodies and a stark white heads. "Those are bald eagles!"

"Yeah, they hang out in the tree line, watching for fish. They like it when the boat churns up the water for 'em."

She whistled low. "Faaan-tastic."

"You never seen one before?"

Madeline shook her head, not taking her eyes off the creatures. Rusty dropped the buoy back into the water, stood, and began rooting through the cabinet. "I got some binoculars here someplace . . ."

A bird came at them, its wings stretching out far longer than Madeline was tall. The eagle's outer feathers, spread like an enormous hand, glowed translucent, highlighted by the morning sun. Seven feet? Eight? Madeline felt her herself gasp, preparing for a scream.

But the bird hit the water next to the boat, with a neat splash and plunk. For a moment, he appeared to be standing, thinking. Then his wings opened up again, and a fish broke the surface, writhing against the raptor's grip. The pair made it only inches from the water when the bird let out a terrible cry and sunk back down again. Flapping, spraying water into the boat, the bird yelled and pulled.

"He's not going to make it," Rusty said. Casually, as if watching someone make a wrong turn.

"What do you mean?"

"That fish is too heavy. See the eagle straining? He's a goner. They can only lift about half their weight."

Madeline felt her heart pound. "Why doesn't he just let go?"

"Can't. Something in the way those birds are made. Once they grip their prey," he bent his right hand into a claw, "they can't let go again until they can stand, you know? They need solid ground." He shrugged. "Sometimes they can swim to shore, but he don't look like he's gonna figure that out."

"Help him!"

Rusty snorted a laugh. "'Nother way to get yourself dead."

Madeline glanced around the boat. Nothing seemed useful. Except maybe the blanket. She could cover the bird and then—

"If he does drown, though, I could stuff him. I could stuff them just the way they are, stuck together like that. That'd bring over a thousand. Man, I gotta get him, got a net around somewheres . . . "

Rusty bent over his cabinet yet again.

Madeline tried to protest but couldn't form words anymore; she only spat muffled sounds of disgust and fury. So she set her hands firm, took a two-step running start and shoved Rusty right off the boat. "What the hell are you—" the rest of his words were dismissed by an extraordinary splash.

He came out of the water sputtering. "You insane? You can't toss me off the boat—I'm the driver!" He sounded more surprised, indeed almost amused, than incensed.

Madeline snatched the blanket, let it drop to unfold. It was a US Navy blanket, blue wool with once-white USN letters along the bottom. Made for a twin bed, judging by the size. Or maybe a cot.

The eagle screeched like a child in a burning building, still flapping uselessly. It would raise an inch or two, be yanked back under two or three.

Madeline stood at the edge of the boat, feet spread wide. She tossed the blanket over the panicked bird, was amazed when it stopped thrashing. She leaned over, wrapped her arms around the quieted beast and heaved.

The weight proved less than she'd anticipated. She tugged harder than she needed to, brought the bundle up too high, and threw herself off balance. She fell backwards. The blanket opened and the fish smacked against her chest. The combined weight of the interlocked animals, maybe twenty pounds, had knocked the wind out of her.

The fish flopped and squirmed on her chest. The eagle's wings raked her face. He bawled right at her, eyes glowing fierce yellow. She tossed her arms up to shield herself. His huge hooked beak pecked at her hat, tore at her arms. She eyed his enormous razor claws and feared for her sight.

The claws flexed. Released the fish. The bird took a step back. She felt its hard talons against her stomach. Felt it push against her to launch.

The eagle flew free. Madeline watched it rise, heard its single, angry shriek. She shoved the fish, flapping and gasping, off her and stumbled to a stand. Blood smarted her eyes; she wiped them and her forehead with her sleeve.

Rusty hollered something, charging back to the boat as best he could through the chest-deep water. She heard only the sound, not the words. She didn't care. She washed her belly, grazed by the eagle's talons even through her sweatshirt, with ocean waters that stung.

Madeline no longer required a lobstering lesson. She knew, lobsterman or not, she would not leave this wild place. She would stay here for good, waiting for her father to return from the war, protected and nurtured by Mother Ocean.

Acknowledgements

The author wishes to thank Ashley Lauren Rogers, NYC playwright and speaker about everything Gender, (also History and Steampunk, if you need those) for helping me fix "High Price of the Wild Truth."

When I first wrote this story, back in 2001, my purpose was to explore and normalize a transgendered woman who was not attempting to "pass." Back then, the mere *fact* of any transgendered woman in a mainstream book seemed progressive. By the time the story was published as part of the novel Survivanoia (2011) that was still mostly true.

Or so the author believed. But a scathing review made me think. And research. Research led me to Ms. Rogers, who leads a workshop in creating (and doing right by) characters who are trans/non-binary gendered.

Publishing a short story collection provided a rare chance to re-visit some already-published work. "High Price of the Wild Truth" fit so well with the theme of the collection, and is about *identity*, it seemed the perfect opportunity to right a wrong. Or *re-write* a wrong, as it were. I hope I've succeeded. I know that if I have it is in large part due to Ms. Rogers.

* * *

On the personal support front, many thanks to all the friends and family who put up with me even when I'm not writing, let alone when I *am*. Special thanks to the Livingstons, the Goods, and my sister Vanessa, who make life fun when it's dreary, and show me I'm more normal than I think.

Extra-special thanks to my husband, Bruce Weinheimer Sr. All those late nights make for a grouchy wife.

About the Author

Baroness Melody Von Smith wrote her first story when she was six. Everybody died in the end. It was a comedy. She is the author of the play *Bonegrinders*, the novel *Survivanoia*. She currently spends most of her time in Western New York where she shares her home with two cats and one husband.

For more information, go to *BaronessVonSmith.com*.